The Queens of the Mines

The Queens of the Mines

Authentic stories which blossomed from
the twisted roots of California.

Written by Andrea Anderson

Youreka! Publishing 2021
ISBN: 9798458777636

For Bella, Sailor, Waylon, Hazel, and Emmi.
You can be, achieve, and gain anything you desire.

The Queen of the Southern Mines

1

With rubber boots on and an umbrella in tow, I left my house for one of the three decaying graveyards within a few blocks from my front steps. It was a quiet, gloomy May morning in the foothills of the Sierra Nevada Mountains. Breaking the silence, dead twigs snapped under my rain boots and raindrops fell off of the leaves of towering oak trees. The creaking of the rusted iron gate rang out, and I stepped back into history. I made my usual first stop, a large monument in the third row. Carved at the top, next to a bundle of calla lilies, read

A. Anderson born 1854, Sweden.

Some of the hand carved grave markers, are easily read, some are worn smooth. None tell me enough about the occupants below. Engraved are faded names alongside birthplaces from over the world, and birth dates dating as far back as the eighteenth century. I keep walking. Bright green moss smothered its own dark and aged growth on the crumbling headstones. Puddles gather and poppies grew where mother nature rattled the earth and father time split the stone causing deep crevices. The weather was odd for that time of year but it felt just right in the misty, historic cemetery.

Standing on a handmade rock wall, I looked down over my town's historic main street. From here, I could see the roof of my house. Washington Street was the eleventh official "main street" in California. It was just steps away from my own bedroom, that settlers who then altered the future of California (and the entire country), rested forever. I have visited these graveyards for over twenty years, attempting to imagine the stories untold of the men and women who risked it all, on a game of chance.

I was born and raised in one of the oldest cities in California. I live in a region incredible enough that people from all around the world seek it as a tourism destination. The waterfalls and rock formations at Yosemite National Park are closer to me than any city, or any town with a shopping mall. My grammar school, high school and the hospital I was born in are literally just footsteps away from the prominent gold mines and historic creek beds that once funded the nation.

In my childhood, it was normal to ride on a horse drawn stagecoach or press my nose to the window of a one hundred year old candy shop, eyeing soft taffy being pulled, and in the winter fresh candy canes would be spun. In the spring, I would watch yelping bandits on horseback lead faux shootouts in the middle of main street and in the summer, there were the annual frog jumps, which were made famous by the past local resident Mark Twain.

On the outskirts of the county, a few miles away in either direction, are Indian Reservations belonging to the descendants of the local native tribes who once kept this land. The Indigenous Sierra Miwok who worked in unity with Mother Earth and cherished, protected and celebrated every inch of the land we now dwell on. Land that would then soon be ravished.

Everywhere you go, reminders are surrounding my community of its burning past and even then, not many of us talk about it. This is where I am from. The Gold Country, Sonora, California, Queen of The Southern Mines.

I am a dream chaser. In my past, I spent a decade as a traveling showgirl and a female empowerment educator. I did this through many forms, most involving dance or performance. In 2017, I was a few years deep touring Europe with my vaudeville show, when a health diagnosis of Ehlers-Danlos Syndrome and POTS, literally took me off my feet. Every aspect of my life immediately changed. Bedridden, I became depressed and shut down.

I was not a stranger to depression after growing up in my father's abusive household. Longing for inspiration, I looked inward. At the age of seventeen, after fifteen years of abuse, my sisters and I had sent my biological father to prison. That was a long time ago. I have three kids now, in the double digits, and he's still in there. I am now estranged from my biological father but I longed to know more about his side of my family tree. My dad's last name was Anderson, and growing up, I would have told you I was half Swedish. Ha.

I found out through a not so deep dive and DNA test, that also on my father's side, I was the granddaughter of generations of strong Native American women. His mother was Cherokee. She lived a hard life working in the lumber mills, and had missing fingers to prove it. She had nine children, an abusive husband and a wicked garden. That was all I could remember.

A grandmother of hers had walked from Georgia to Oklahoma on The Trail of Tears and later made her way to California. My third great aunt Rebecca Tickanesky Neugin, was the last living person who had made the treacherous journey known as The Trail of Tears. I also found my four time great grandmother who came from Nicaragua, and helped settle Mokelumne Hill. I recently found her grave. She was a working part of the California Gold Rush and she lived right here, right where I grew up. I had no idea.

In our California elementary school textbooks, we learned many white men's names and read their glorified stories. When California was first made a state, white women were scarce and the Native, Mexican and Central American population who lived there were mostly left undocumented and unaccounted for. We do know that the population of white females only rose from three percent to eight percent during the entire gold rush.

It all led me to wonder, what was it like for the women here in the 1850s? What hardships did they face and what victories were they able to realize? Who were the first women who came to California and who was already here? I embarked on a search to learn what life was like for women like my great-grandmothers.

I began to map out a historical fiction novel I would write about my hometown. The more I learned about the history, and researched real people from the time, I began to connect in deep ways with the lives of ten brilliant people who made their own way in a time where women were not so welcome to do so. In the lessons I learned, I myself, struck gold. The stories contributed to the shaping of the future of California and the United States. They are rarely heard about, and I want you to know their names.

Britton & Rey, Lithographer, and George H Goddard. Sonora from the north / G. H. Goddard, del. Lith. Britton & Rey, San Francisco. California Sonora, 1853. Sonora: Published by G. S. Wells, May. Photograph. https://www.loc.gov/item/2011661680/

C. H. Goddard del.
Lith. Britton & Rey San Francisco
SONORA FROM THE NORTH.
Published by G. S. Wells, Sonora

Mexican Alta California

2

Before America's largest migration, the gold rush, Mexican Alta California or Nueva California was inhabited by the Native California Indian tribes and the Mexican ranchers that were referred to as the Californios. There were a few white settlers in the region, mostly American citizens who had traveled from the East. They were by far the minority. The Californios were not connected to, or working with the government in Mexico City, you could say that Alta California was "off the grid".

California's indigenous people spoke up to ninety different languages. The Spanish language followed and just before the gold rush, the majority of the population was speaking Spanish. For its size, Mexican Alta California was the most linguistically diverse area of North America. In 1849, in the first California State Constitution, it was stated that "all laws must be published in Spanish and English". From its birth into the nation and for three more decades, California was made to be bilingual.

A day's ride west from the Motherlode, resting quietly in the fog, was the sleepy bay village of Yerba Buena. It was once a busy port town whose population had diminished after the Canadian fur trading empire "The Hudson Bay Company" had sold its holdings and left. When that happened, most of the community followed.

Yerba Buena's name was changed to San Francisco. There, in poorly built canvas tents and hand crafted shacks, less than eight hundred people resided. The Californios Mexican miners and ranchers settled on the land that was further into the foothills of the Sierra Nevada Mountains. My home town Sonora was first called Sonoran Camp, named by the miners who settled the town after migrating up from Sonora, Mexico. This is of course after the Miwok, who was already here.

In 1776, under the direction of Father Junipero Serra, the Mission Dolores in San Francisco was established and the buildings were then built by Native labor. It was one of twenty-one established along California's coastal towns.

At the Missions, the California Indians were forced into converting to Catholicism. For seventy-three years, the objective was "saving souls," but sadly, it was literally only the soul they were trying to save. The quality of life while the Indigenous person was alive was of no concern. If they were to die sooner, it was just another soul sent to heaven, saved.

The friars whipped, beat, burned and tortured their captives and when the Natives died and the workforce lessened, they ventured out for new blood.

Yet, some remaining "converted" California Indians continued to willingly live at Pueblo Dolores after the cultural disruption, among the nearly five thousand of their people who were buried there.

On the coast of California, surviving natives were most likely forcefully converted to catholicism and doing back breaking labor for the Spanish missions or at a private ranch. They were most likely underfed, overworked, and sick or dying from the diseases brought by the fair skinned newcomers. Before the colonization by Spain, Russia and Mexico, there were over 300,000 Native Americans living in what would be known as California. Just before America's largest migration, the Gold Rush, only one hundred and fifty-thousand remained.

In the foothills, the Native Tribes survived on nature's bounty. The men hunted rabbits and deer, and pulled a variety of fish and shellfish from the nearby waters while the women collected berries, roots, acorns, and fruit. Working with the changing winds, the tribes moved to where the food was plentiful and shelter was accessible, season to season, place to place, unaware of the horrors that lay just ahead.

New Helvetia

3

At the crossing of the American and Sacramento rivers, a self proclaimed displaced Swiss military officer with a french passport, stood watching a group of his working men on the fifty-thousand acres on which he stood. The land was granted to him by Juan Bautista Alvarado, the Las Californias Governor in an effort to diminish American encroachment on Mexico's territory. The deal was made under one condition, that the man became a Mexican citizen. On his way to California through the Sandwich Islands (Hawaii) and upon arrival, this man had captured or bought nearly eight hundred islanders and the local indigenous. He began to build an agricultural kingdom. Orchards and vineyards were planted. A fort was built.

He came to the river that winter morning to check in with James, the hired white man overseeing the work. James was frustrated and bitter towards the sweating enslaved men. They had dug the ditch too shallow, which caused water to back up under the current project, creating a disaster. The boss's thumb rested on a small patch of dark hair under his bottom lip as he stroked his mustache, eyebrows furrowed. This mistake would put them back for months. Steaming, the boss stomped back to his homestead on the property.

This man was not a displaced officer. He was a wanted man, and he had been on the run for 15 years. His name was Johann August Suter. Suter had left his wife, five children and an enormous debt he could not repay behind and fled Switzerland. He used a more American sounding version of his name, once arriving in California. John Sutter.

John Sutter would have to make a new plan with James Marshall, who had been supervising the men who were working their lives away building an empire for John Sutter that he called Sutter's Fort.

It would have been a devastating life if you were one of the female California Indians living under Sutter's rule. As a punishment for your race and gender, you would surely endure recurring rape and violence. Your children would possibly be stolen and sold off or even given away as gifts. You would be punished by violence if you attempted to escape.

In an unwilling exchange of your fire warmed hut, you now would sleep on a cold stone floor without bedding. No more beautiful ceremonies. Now separated from you, these discouraged men who once stood tall and proud, could no longer gather with you to enjoy bountiful meals from nature with your own hands. Instead, you knelt over a crowded trough under the blistering sun to fight for the thin porridge they called 'sic'.

You would work with no reward, with the exception of John Sutter's scraps of tin, redeemable only at his store. How generous, of this American "*hero*"? I want to take a quick pause long enough to say that these men do not star in this series. This dreary story will soon bloom with incredible color, but California's history is like a poppy field. Below vibrant gardens, twisted roots grow, buried in the dark.

There was a knock at John Sutter's door, then another. The shuffling of pure anticipation came from outside the hatchway. Sutter set his book down on the chair near his bed and moved across the room as the rapping grew louder and more persistent. Sutter yelled, "*I am coming god dammit*". The knocking stopped as he opened the door, revealing a large grin under the unkempt beard of an impatient James Marshall.

Marshall had just finished inspecting the channel below the water mill for slits and debris on a chilly January morning in 1848. He had now arrived back at camp, bearing stunning news for his boss. Minutes later they both sat quietly staring in awe at what sat tucked away in a cloth in Marshall's hand. After testing it, they knew for certain. It was gold. From right there, in the American River.

Marshall silently watched his boss pace back and forth. Sutter had one hand on hip and one hand fingering his facial hair. His mind was racing. "Surely it would be detrimental," he said, "if word spread about this find." He faced out the window and envisioned his land overtaken with gold-seeking men, destroying his agricultural empire in the making. All would be lost. With that devastating thought in mind, Sutter and Marshall set a plan into motion to keep this discovery silent. In the mean time, Sutter attempted to acquire as much of the surrounding land as possible.

Two years earlier, in 1846, the ship Brooklyn brought a Mormon group leader with 238 Saints. They intended to start their own self sufficient colony. His entourage of carpenters, blacksmiths, farmers, bakers and everything a community might need, had doubled or tripled the population of San Francisco. With him, he brought a printing press and used it to publish San Francisco's first newspaper, The Alta.

His large group settled Mormon Island on the Sacramento Delta and quickly jumpstarted the local economy. When the Mormon leader abandoned his post on the California Star newspaper in Yerba Buena, he opened a store in New Helvetia. Right next to Sutter's Fort, on the Sacramento River. The leaders name was Sam Brannan. Four months after Marshall's discovery, Brannan had made his own find, and was busy putting his own plan into motion. With gold he had found and stored in a glass jar, he traveled to San Francisco. He famously paraded up and down the streets of the port town yelling "*Gold! Gold! Gold! From the American River!*" Before you could even imagine, the city was nearly empty as the settlers hastily pressed to Fort Sutter. So that's that. That is how it started. Sam Brannan then began his success story as California's first millionaire. Considering, before his big announcement, he first established the store with all of the mining equipment and supplies that would obviously remain in hot demand.

Sutter's own story did not end with as much accomplishment. Just as he had feared, his land was indeed ravished and everything of his was in fact, lost. Furthermore, the news of gold beyond imagination was spreading like a California wildfire. There was an unimaginable number of people on their way. It seemed as if the entire world was rushing to California, and men were not the only pioneers with stars in their eyes. Frontier pioneer Eliza Inman wrote in her journal in 1843, "*If Hell laid to the West, Americans would cross Heaven to reach it.*"
It looks like she was right.

My Friend Swifty
4

By 2018, I was learning how to work from home, and had recently started researching gold rush characters for a historical fiction novel that I intended on writing. My best friend Sarah was living across the street. Sarah was in a nineteenth century US History class at UC Merced and had been writing a paper titled the *Mythology of the Mother Lode*.

Sarah is a good teacher. While studying together on my front porch, it became clear to me how one's race, gender, and the related labor restrictions could hinder one's chance at "hitting the motherlode." I truly saw that the modern collective memory of the Ol' West, was often romanticized. She informed me that even though it was in fact, a wide open land that was ripe with resources and endless possibilities that were ready to be conquered and claimed, BUT not by just *any* individual who was ambitious, strong and persistent enough to brave the terrain. There is VERY little mention of the non white male experience.

Sarah was studying old newspaper archives. She would call, text, or run across the street to my house to share her findings. We found clear examples of racism against the Mexican, Black, Chinese, and Native people who were living locally and across the country. What better documented the beliefs, values, norms, traditions, politics and social settings than the newspapers of the time?

One morning over five cups of coffee, both bundled in bath robes, Sarah showed me the 1865 winter issue of The Mariposa Gazette. The issue clearly demonstrated how the Native California Indians were being devalued. In addition to several brief reports of "killing Indians," the article that we both found most disturbing was a front page story consuming upwards the entirety of the page. It was a detailed account of Yosemite's beauty. It seemed sweet. Until you read on and the writer boasted, "No white man had ever looked upon its sublime wonders until 1851, when we came here in pursuit of Indians… coming to kill and exterminate." It stuck with me, and I think about it all the time. If you are a person that visits Yosemite, or plans to, the next time you are there, I hope you can find your own way to honor the lives lost. The lives of those who were the original keepers of one of our planet's most beautiful gifts.

The Placer Herald casually mentioned a lynching a black man at Beal's Bar for stealing a watch. Illustrating the casualness and normality of the devaluation of Chinese people, the Chinese locals were referred to in the paper as "Celestials" or "Moon-eyed Devils". We read President Johnson's statement, and you can imagine the weight of glorifying these words from ya know, the President.

"I should try to introduce negro suffrage. Gradually, first to those who have served in the army, those who could read and write and perhaps a property qualification of $200. It will not do to let black people have universal suffrage now."

There was a proclaimed "success story" of a merchant living in Philadelphia who had a 5223 acre plantation in Cuba. A third of the property was planted in cane, producing 4.1 million pounds of sugar, and 131,000 gallons of molasses a year, which sold in the US for 147,000 dollars. The spending power of over 5 million dollars in 2022. The merchant had low overhead and high profit. Why such a low expense for such a huge production? Well, I read on, he had four hundred and fifty-seven slaves, three hundred of whom he considered "effective". They each manufactured 12,532 pounds a year.

Shortly after the 13th amendment was ratified, abolishing slavery, the Gazette reported that, "There will be no more wrangling over the fugitive slave laws; no quarrels over the slavery question." Obviously suggesting that prior to this, California might not have been as free of a state as they say.

While California territory was part of Mexico Under Mexican law, and when California declared statehood in 1850, the land had long been declared free soil. But here we were, reading a newspaper from 15 years later that was claiming that the slavery quarrel was *finally* resolved. Stacy Smith's *Freedom's Frontier* explains that slavery existed in California. Mexico coerced their peons. Rancheros long captured and enslaved Natives and wealthy Chinese men conquered both Chinese men and women. Many Americans brought their slaves with them out west, and captured Natives in pursuit of fortune.

The place of a woman was simply proven in the birth announcements from the same newspaper, which never mentioned the names of the mother of the newborn, instead she was always referred to as, "The wife of." Another jarring example in the same edition read "females cannot be employed at National banks on account of them not being citizens". In case you had not realized that women, as non-citizens, were simply not immediately entitled to the rewards of the West.

In the early nineteenth century the "cult of true womanhood" and the "separate spheres philosophy" were creeds that were generally followed by white and Protestant families. Social prejudice excluded the working class, immigrants, and blacks from the rules. The "cult of true womanhood" theory bound women to four fundamental morals: piety, purity, domesticity, and submissiveness.

Everything was split into two separate spheres between men and women, the public life and private life. The spheres did not overlap. Women served and obeyed the husband and managed the household and the children in the private sphere. The woman was to practice morality and teach her family religion. The public sphere included politics, commerce, and the law. This was considered the men's responsibility, for women were considered childlike and unable to make decisions.

The excerpts from the newspapers revealed that white men were not ready nor interested in opening the labor market to women or people of color. This was tolerated because there was great benefit of this system. Clearly, this left limited access for upward mobility for any free Female, Black, Native, Mexican and Chinese that lived in California at the time. They would have to discover alternative economic opportunities and work to defend themselves against a great effort to render them defenseless.

The papers we read revealed a severe contrast of narrative than the folklore we hear of today. Many of us have accepted the history we were taught as truth without challenge. Despite the tales of success for "anyone" who worked hard enough, the West was actually quite limited.

Sarah, by the way, graduated from UC Merced with highest honors, and she greatly affected the direction in which I was writing, researching, and understanding the Gold Rush. Fictional novel out, true stories in. Thank you Sarah, from this small town American girl. You made me realize the stories that remain through the years are usually those of the people in power. That the undermined people are often rendered voiceless, leaving them ghosts of our past, dismissed and forgotten.

There is an African Proverb, I am reminded of often while reviewing the history of the US. It says, *"Until the story of the hunt is told by the lion, the tale of the hunt will always glorify the hunter."*

Tax
5

The Mexican American War started in 1846, and the defeat of the Mexican army, fall of Mexico City and the surrender of their government came in 1847. In 1848, peace negotiations were made when the Treaty of Guadalupe Hidalgo was signed. The Treaty of Guadalupe Hidalgo ended the Mexican American War in favor of the United States.

The United States paid Mexico $15 million dollars and agreed to squash all of the claims their citizens had against Mexico. Fifty percent of Mexico territory was handed over to the United States, including Nevada, Utah, New Mexico, most of Arizona parts of Wyoming and all of California. Months later, the Gold Rush began.

So, the American and other white immigrants felt superior to the experienced miners from Mexico who moved up north and found success in transporting supplies to the mines and locating profitable claims. This resulted in an anti-Mexican sentiment. Despite the guarantees by the Treaty extended to the Spanish speaking residents.

Was Manifest Destiny an ego syndrome?

Peter H. Burnett was the first Governor of the state of California. Raised in a slave owning family, Burnett was among those who founded Oregon City in Butte County. There, he authored the infamous "Burnett's lash law." The law allowed flogging any free black person who refused to leave the town.

When Peter H. Burnett made his way to the Bay Area, he met John Augustus Sutter Jr, the son of John Sutter. Sutter Jr was selling his father's deeded lands in the near vicinity of Sutter's Fort. He offered Burnett a job selling land plots for the new town of Sacramento. Within a year, Burnett had earned fifty thousand dollars (over $1.8 million in 2022).

Peter H. Burnett was then appointed to serve on the first Supreme Court of California. He was an owner of two slaves. When calls were made to make California a slave state, he opposed. Burnett instead pushed for the *total* exclusion of African-Americans in California.

Burnett signed the Foreign Miners Tax Act in the spring of 1850 in an effort to eliminate Mexican competition in the mines. The Act stated that all non US citizen miners in California were to pay a monthly fee of twenty dollars to work their own claims. That would be the equivalent of seven hundred and twenty-one United States dollars in 2022. Per Month.

Of that twenty dollars, the tax collector would keep three and the rest would be remitted to the state. In consequence of this tax, miners of color were subjected to both legalized and mob-inspired discrimination and persecution. Mexicans, Chinese and Native Americans were being forced to leave the area. It was suggested that there was no room for anyone considered foreign in California or it's mines that were worth millions of dollars of gold.

It was May of 1850, one month after the Foreign Miners' Tax had passed when a flame for protest sparked in Sonora, California. Along Woods Creek and beyond, miners were raising their nations' flags over their camps as a couple French and Spanish speaking miners posted this notice around the county.

"It is time to unite: Frenchmen, Chileans, Peruvians, Mexicans, there is the biggest necessity of putting an end to the vexation of the Americans in California. If you do not intend to allow yourself to be fleeced by a band of miserable fellows who are repudiated by their own country, then unite and go to the camp of Sonora next Sunday: there will we try to guarantee security for us all, and put a bridle in the mouths of that horde who call themselves citizens of the United States, thereby profaning that country."

On Saturday, May 18, 1850, Frenchmen patrolled around Sonora, armed to the teeth. That night, an American, representing himself a Collector approached a Chilean mans home and demanded the tax. The Chilean man told the American he did not have enough money to pay. The American told him "Then you must quit work". When the man quietly left his hole, the American jumped into it in his place. Exasperated, the Chilean man cut the jugular vein of the American and he died in a few minutes. Word spread to Mormon Gulch and Jamestown and within hours, about four hundred Americans were there remaining until the next day.

Sunday, May 19, 1850, known as the last day of grace given by the Collector and the day of "The Resistance to the Tax on Foreigners" protest in Tuolumne County.

A group of about four thousand mostly Mexican and Peruvian miners led by two exiled French miners protested against the tax in the plaza of Sonora that morning. They were chased by a volunteer militia made up of nearly five hundred tax collectors and alarmed American miners.

A Mexican man was killed on the spot by the Sheriff's deputy after he a knife and killed the newly elected county sheriff. This caused the American miners to turn out en masse. Over one hundred of the foreigners were arrested. The protest ended when the Anglos raised their rifles and fired on the rebels. For several days a painful suspense prevailed with either side all in readiness to march at a moment's warning to the assistance of their fellow citizens. These rebel "foreign" miners drafted a statement to the governor, saying they would accept a lower tax of four or five dollars.

It was reported that it was in fact the foreigners in Tuolumne County that presented such strong resistance, no doubt contributed to the change in the next tax laws. A Sonora miner wrote, "It nearly became a war of extermination."

Downieville
6

Major William Downie first heard of the discovery of gold in California at the Love Joy Hotel in Buffalo NY. He arrived in San Francisco on June 27, 1849. The ship's entire crew abandoned their work and ran with the passengers for the foothills.

Major Downie's company was made up of ten Black sailors, an older Irish man and a young MeWuk man who they met on the trail. He joined in the excursion to provide knowledge of the land and skills in the unknown terrain. They headed to the northern mines, stopping on the upper North Fork of the Yuba River.
Here, Major William Downie wrote in his journal.

"The hillsides were covered with oaks, bending their crooked branches in fantastic forms, while here and there a mighty pine towered above them, and tall willows waved their slender branches, as it were, nodding us a welcome."

That December, Downie and company moved into a rustic log cabin they had built high above the river at "The Forks". The erection of this structure gave Downie cause to claim to be the founder of what he called Downieville. As the men settled in for the cold, they discovered they had a single bottle of brandy left. For what was almost a week, the men argued for over whether to drink it on Christmas, or New Year's Eve.

The anxious men eventually agreed on the sooner holiday. On Christmas, the men got drunk off of an anticipated moment and a punch of brandy mixed with hot water and nutmeg. It wasn't long before Downie climbed onto the cabin roof, with a flag and a pistol.

Back to his journal,

"I made a short speech, waved the flag, and fired a few shots and finished up by giving three cheers for the American Constitution. Merry Christmas."

Revenge
7

Holding her long black wool skirt up to not trip, a young woman shuffled quickly down a busy street. She passed by men who hollered out at her, some uttered threats under their breath. She approached the end of the street to her makeshift cabin that rested among giant evergreens and golden poppies. She quickly shut the door behind her. As she rested against the door, her vision began to blur. Her face tingled like one hundred sewing needles pierced her face. The crown of her head dripped with sweat. Her breasts were on fire. She moved to the kitchen area and collapsed near a tin bowl on the floor, and vomited into it.

Josefa Segovia carefully stood up, and cupping her belly, she looked out the window. She knew she was with child, although it was too soon to show. Another reason to protect herself. The last thing she needed was dealing with rebuffing his sexual advances once again. The young woman grabbed a Bowie knife from the back of the house, went to her bed, and slid it under the blanket she had rolled up to use as a pillow. In Downieville, property and dark skinned women's bodies were like gold, anyones for the taking.

She was one of three Mexican women in town, it was July 4, 1851, the first Independence Day for California.

Downieville was buzzing with townspeople participating in the town's favorite pastime, two fisted drinking. Gambling halls and the drinking establishments were swarmed with miners. Children in patriotic outfits screeched up and down the streets with excitement. Later, they would all cheer as a parade passed through town, followed by a speech from the governor, Peter H. Burnett.

Jack Craycroft's Gambling Palace was busier than usual, and twenty year old barmaid Josefa Segovia could hardly keep up with her duties. Hustling through the saloon with a tray of whiskey glasses, she passed by her boyfriend Jose who was dealing Monte. Josefa rolled her eyes and gave him a wink. A smile crept across the man's face. He was roughly dressed compared to the white men in the bar, who were in their best for the occasion.

The couple had lived in Downieville for the past six months after working in mining towns, first traveling up from Sonora, Mexico, through the Sonora Camp in Tuolumne, then to Downieville. They had both secured work at Jack Craycroft's Gambling Palace, and were very much in love.

As if Josefa wasn't busy and bothered enough during this shift, the day grew worse when *he* walked in. *He* looked especially flashy today, and he stood even prouder than usual, which says a lot considering that he stood well over six feet tall and considering his boasting ego. In a generous mood, he began buying drinks all around. *He* was Frederick Cannon, commonly known as Jock. It had been nearly a week since Josefa had received a warning from a friend of Jose, who had overheard Jock discussing his plan to break into her home to defile her, yet again. Josefa attempted to stay out of Jock's sight and tried to get Jose's attention, who was too caught up in his game to notice.

Jock's voice echoed through the hall, singing with his pal Oregon. Josefa didn't mind Oregon, she actually liked him, when he wasn't around Jock. It didn't take long for Jock to notice Josefa, and he began ordering all of his drinks through her. He took pleasure in running her ragged. Josefa's refusal to make eye contact with Jock began to anger the Scotsman. He had a weakness for the woman, which he displayed to his friends and to her, as hatred.

Josefa needed to catch her breath for the first time during her busy shift and took a seat safely next to Jose at his monte table. Drunk, Jock paced the bar looking for Josefa and approached the Monte game, demanding a drink while grabbing her bare shoulder. Josefa was out of her chair in one move, whipping the Bowie knife from her black wool garter. She stood facing Jock, blade in hand. Josefa was ready. Oregon, hearing the commotion, crossed the room and quickly pulled Jock away.

It seemed as if the scuffle was over, but as Josefa watched Oregon drag Jock out of Jack Craycroft's Gambling Palace, Jock's eyes met hers, and they told otherwise.

Under a bright moon, Jock, Oregon, and another friend stumbled through the streets of Downieville, raising hell in the early morning hours on the fifth of July. The men were yelling into the night sky, banging on doors and kicking rocks in a stupor. When the men approached the Segovia's cabin under the evergreens, they knew Josefa was at home and they knew Jose was still at work.

Inside, Josefa was awake. She couldn't sleep that night, and was already in the kitchen when Jock kicked her door down and solely entered the home as his friends stood guard outside. The towering man began moving towards her bed, Josefa managed to surprise Cannon from behind. He leapt at her and he wrestled her to the floor, Jock groping and Josefa pushing him off until Jock's gang called to him from on the porch, and they all ran off into the night.

It was especially hot in Downieville the next morning after the state's first Independence Day and many miners were still in celebration mode, hungover and roaming the streets, finding shade under the towering oaks or finding much needed relief in the refreshing river that ran through the Sierra Nevada Mountains.

Jock, still drunk, stumbled up to the home of Josefa and Jose. He stood in front of the cabin and yelled to the exposed doorway for Josefa to come out. Instead, Jose appeared in the door frame, and he was pissed. Jose immediately demanded payment for breaking his door the night before. An argument ensued, and other still drunk patriotic miners gathered to see what looked as though would become a brawl.

Josefa stormed out of the home and positioned herself between the two men. She stood under the tall man, looking up at him, yet down at him at the same time. She and Cannon continued the argument in Spanish, in which he continued to berate her. When he called her a whore, she dared Cannon to come into her house and say those words again. Jock followed her into the home and immediately put his hands on her, with breath stinking of whiskey. "You know you are just a Mexican whore." Moments later, the quiet waiting crowd saw Fredrick Jock Cannon stagger out of the open doorway, clutching his bleeding chest. She screamed at him in Spanish that she was not a whore as he bled out on the ground in front of her home.

Josefa Segovia, had stabbed Fredrick Jock Cannon in the heart with her Long Bowie knife, clear through his sternum bone. The cry of murder rang through Downieville, and Josefa's fate was soon to be determined by the hostility of this proud, mostly white community.

Josefa and Jose rushed through their home and out the back door. They ran along the footpath towards Jack Craycroft's Gambling Palace, never looking back. Her heart was pounding furiously in her chest, her face hot, the sound of Jock's cracking sternum repeating in her head. They burst through the door of the saloon in a panic. A few local Mexican men, friends of theirs, were gambling inside and were startled by their distress. The men quickly agreed to try to protect and hide the couple.

Downstairs, Josefa rocked in Jose's embrace, unsure of what was to come as an angry mob formed outside. The blood thirsty miners banged on the locked doors and shouted threats. They would tear down the saloon if the men continued to withhold the woman. Her friends secured the bar until the door of Craycroft's Palace was beaten down. A group of men entered and pulled the Mexican gamblers harboring the couple outside for a beating. The rest searched Craycroft's. Josefa was found hiding with Jose behind a barrel and captured. Two tall Scottish men dragged the screaming Mexican woman and her lover into the street. The mob was tightening around them, cursing, spitting and throwing blows at her and Jose until the two were taken into custody and placed in an empty building.

The town of Downieville was isolated, far from the center of law, order and protection. Josefa would face a miner's trial with the law in the hands of the screaming and seething mob, who had all celebrated together as American citizens the night before. Consumed in a patriotic hangover, the angry town was full of racial tension. Josefa watched from the cracks in the walls as the crowd swelled from six hundred to three thousand white men. The trial was set within an hour.

They felt the act was tragic, shameful, and that Josefa had gone too far. An attorney who whole-heartedly believed in Josefas' defense took his role seriously and worked quickly to save her, despite the pushback from the townspeople. The platform that had been erected for the Fourth of July celebration was used as a makeshift courtroom. Jock's cold body was displayed on exhibit, his shirt cut open to reveal the bloody, fatal chest wound.

The crowd silenced as Jock Cannon's friends were brought to the platform to give their testimony. One by one, they explained their version of the breaking down of the door, and the confrontation that ended in Jock's death. Oregon told the crowd, with his hat on his chest, they only innocently knocked on the door, and it had just fallen down, with the lightest tap. The crowd went crazy, Josefa watched the faces of the men grow angrier with her. She was in a rage of disbelief. To think she once admired this man.

Oregon went on to tell the engaged mob, when it fell, they had just set the door back up and left, pulling Jock away from the cabin. When Jock had returned in the morning, his only intention to apologize to Josefa for his earlier behavior and fix the door. The silence again turned to a growing mumbling grew as Jose approached the stand. Jose was not given the same respect from the mob as he stated that he had heard Cannon call Josefa a whore, and continued his verbal abuse following her into their home. Jose was quickly ushered off the platform and Josefa was brought up. It was hard to hear her broken English over the mob's shouting.

Josefa spoke on how she had become afraid of Jock Cannon, admitting to even sleeping with a knife under her pillow. She told of previous interactions she had with Jock, rebuffing his aggressive sexual abuse from time and time again in the past. She explained how she had received a warning from some of the Mexican boys in town who had overheard him discussing breaking into her house to attempt to rape the young woman, again. Josefa Segovia admitted to killing Cannon with the knife, yet insisted she had acted in self-defense. Josefa was not heard.

Anyone else who wanted to speak on behalf of Josefa was quickly thrown off the platform, or simply not allowed up to begin with. In one last attempt, her defense lawyer brought doctor Cyrus D. Aiken to examine Segovia in the miner's cabin she had been held in. After the examination, the doctor testified that Josefa was indeed at least three-months pregnant. He demanded from the platform that her innocent child should not suffer for the sins of its mother, and that a pregnancy, or even the possibility of one, should delay any trial resulting in an execution.

The angry mob demanded Josefa to be examined by another doctor in town, this time, in plain view of the mob. The chosen doctor was known to be dishonest, and after a public inspection, he disagreed with the diagnosis that Dr. Aiken had given Josefa. He insisted that she was not pregnant. Dr. Aiken was given just two hours to get out of town, he obeyed and vanished. He was never to be seen in Downieville again.

Josefa's lawyer, refusing to lose, stood on a barrel reciting a passionate speech and begging for a second chance for Josefa and her unborn child. The barrel he stood on was furiously kicked out from under him. As he scrambled to find his eye glasses and his hat, he was lifted up by the men and hauled off hundreds of yards away. He received a severe beating, and told to stay back. Next, Jose was forcefully escorted out of town.

A jury of white men from Downieville wasted no time in finding Josefa guilty of murder, and sentenced her to be hung then and there. In the last two hours of her life, Josefa was taken home to pick out an outfit to die in and rushed back to wait in the hot empty building. As she dressed for her hanging, through a slit in the wall, she watched a group of men build a scaffold off of the Jersey Bridge over the Yuba River. It was a double A-frame construction with a cribbed pier made of gathered logs and filled with boulders.

Josefa stood tall, wearing the red, finest hoop skirt she possessed. Climbing the steps of her gallows, as if walking a parade, she shoved her Panama hat into Oregon's chest without making eye contact. The Sheriff asked Josefa if she had anything to say for herself. She shot back. "Nothing, but I would do the same thing again if I was so provoked." The crowd was momentarily shocked into silence. An eagle watched from a limb above the bridge as Josefa went on. "Be sure my remains are decently taken care of". As she said this, she raised her long, loose tresses carefully in order to fix the rope firmly in its place, she adjusted the noose to her own neck. The still-silent crowd stood, jaws dropped as she bravely handled the rope herself.

Before the pistol could even be fired to signal the men to cut the lashings, with a smile and a wave of her hand to the bloodthirsty crowd, Josefa shouted "Adiós Señors" and stepped calmly from the plank into eternity. The lynching then ended with Josefa's lifeless body enduring a severe beating by several men. Her body was tossed from one another as they took their turn. This is how the pregnant Josefa Segovia died, after being hanged from a bridge in Downieville on July 5, 1851. Josefa was one of only twenty-five women out of a population of over five thousand men. She was the first, last and only woman lynched in California.

The Daily Alta California reported, "She did not exhibit the least fear," and the Dogtown Territorial Quarterly proclaimed the woman "bravely faced her fate." Her death was soon quickly condemned around the state. Nine days later, Daily Alta California called it a "blot upon the history of the State". San Francisco newspapers reported that it was outrageous, "That a community would kill a woman where women were so scarce." Josefa was denied the moral, physical and emotional protection a white woman would expect at the time. "It was not her guilt which condemned this unfortunate woman," one journalist wrote, "but her Mexican blood".

The dirt at the Downieville Cemetery was very hard to dig in July. The man who was hired to dig the graves for Josefa and Jock had struggled for the entire day. He eventually decided to spare himself the extra labor and made one large grave, which he rolled Jock and Josefa's wooden caskets into. The two enemies shared a grave in the old Downieville cemetery for nineteen years.

Three feet deep into the frozen earth, two men quickly dug, without speaking a word. A sliver of the moon, barely gleamed over the scene. The sound of two shovels clashing and dirt being moved was all that could be heard on that extra dark night, in the small graveyard in Downieville, California. Now standing waist deep in a grave that had been dug for two, a sudden creak and shift startled the two men. The larger man awkwardly crawled out and laid onto his stomach, his face peering down in the hole.

He strained his eyes in the pitch black to watch his friend sift through the soft dirt with a handkerchief held over his face. Looking up, he motioned for the oil lamp that sat on the headstone, next to the dug up unmarked grave. Lowering the light to the open wooden casket and decomposed remains, the man revealed a red wool skirt, and took the decomposed body's skull from its grave. The skull of Josefa

Segovia. Later, the skull sat on a stand, on a piece of red velvet. The men's club that the grave robbers belonged to, stood around the skull, preparing for a secret initiation. A secret concoction was poured into the skull, it was passed around, and drank out of during the ceremony.

The ghost of Josefa Segovia was believed to be roused in 1870 when the cemetery was moved so greedy miners could look for gold in the hard dirt. It has been reported that her spirit haunts the south-east corner of the Jersey Bridge in Downieville, and she calls to the living on foggy nights. She has been seen as a ghostly figure walking along the bridge as a fog shape of a human, or a face surrounded by her billowing hair. Some say she speaks, but you cannot hear the words she so desperately tries to get across. The original Jersey bridge was destroyed in a flood ten years after her lynching, and was then rebuilt. The Craycroft building still stands today. A plaque dedicated to Segovia's memory by the ECV is near the bridge where she was hanged. It refers to her only as Juanita, even though records of the time give her full and real name. And if you want to know anymore about skulls and secret rituals, you will have to do your own kind of digging.

"Always think of the Spanish girl standing on the plank of a bridge, tossing her hat to a friend and putting a rope around her neck, folding her hands and facing death with a bravery that shamed us men"

- Franklin Buck

Artist's impression of Segovia's hanging, from William Downie's *Hunting for Gold*, published 1893

Distraction

8

The soles of young Arabella Ryan's satin boots were wearing thin from today's pacing. It was now dusk, and she was still wandering hopelessly. She looked down at her tired, aching feet on the dusty street. She had not been paying attention to where she was going. It didn't matter, she had nowhere to go.

She stopped at a bench in front of a white picket fence, and with a sigh of surrender, sank down onto it. A river of tears followed. On the otherwise silent street in New Orleans, for hours, the sobs of a lonely seventeen year old echoed in the night. Her heart was completely empty, like the purse that hung motionless at her side. She had sewn the small bag at the dress shop back in Baltimore, Maryland where she had worked as a seamstress with her younger sister, living a simple and pure life. She was raised by her father, an honest, strict and wise minister. Her mother was soft spoken, doting and dedicated.

It had been a month since Arabella arrived in New Orleans by stagecoach. She had fled home with an older lover when her pregnancy, conceived out of wedlock, was discovered. She was left disowned by her god-fearing parents. The plan was to start a family in New Orleans, where her partner had secured a room for them in a boarding house.

Arabella's mind wandered back to the day she was told to leave, a knot formed in her stomach. Her mother and sisters' tears soaked her cheeks after their quick embrace. She stood in front of her father, who shook his head, staring past her. His eyes, vacant from any past memory of admiration for his daughter. His face when he closed the door on her for the last time, still impaled her.

Arabella had never been on her own before. She had put her new life into the hands of her gentleman lover. After Arabella gave birth to their child, she came home to nothing. The man she loved and trusted had left, and never came back. Now on random bench in New Orleans, the innocent Miss Ryan was left devastated. She was alone, no parents, no little sister, no lover, and after yesterday morning at the Charity Hospital in New Orleans, no baby.

Arabella finally calmed down enough to catch her breath and sat up straight to compose herself. Pushing a dark curly lock of hair behind her ear. Laying her head back, she looked up to the early morning sky and exhaled, asking for an answer. Was this chain of events made to be a punishment for her sins? Or was it the opposite? Arabella had never allowed herself to imagine a life outside of Baltimore before this last month. Was she getting a second chance? She sat there and contemplated the idea of a blank slate. Would there be more ahead for her life? More to come of her story? The sound of footsteps broke her concentration. She snapped her head down and looked around the empty street. No one was there. A strict but safe voice rang out from behind her. "Have you finished crying?" The woman this voice belonged to, recognized the pain of the young girl in shambles in front of her successful bawdy house. She had waited until four in the morning for her to purge Arabella tears, then hired her on the spot.

Arabella's skills as a seamstress were utilized by repairing and sewing dresses for the ladies of the house. The dresses she repaired were unlike anything she herself had ever tried on. Gowns extravagant in design, rouged, tasseled and sensual in cut. Some exposed the shoulders and the ladies full ankle. Some even up to the mid calf!

The Madame had invested in beautiful imported fabrics and trimming and the women decorated the home in a rainbow of opulent gowns. The best of the best was insisted on in her emporium of sin and men came from miles away to socialize in such a lavish setting. Arabella admired the woman for her business savvy, and took note.

Arabella Ryan began gathering courage early into the first few weeks of her employment. She realized that the women wearing these luxurious dresses were carrying heavier purses than the girl sitting in the back room sewing them. Arabella insisted on changing her position in the finest parlor house bordello in New Orleans. When I say change positions, I mean literally.

Arabella Ryan adjusted the stockings on her voluptuous thighs. Using a small thin compact mirror, she checked the rouge on her cheeks before leaving her upstairs quarters. She traced her dainty gloved hand along the brass banister of the grand staircase. Descending the staircase, she scanned the sea of gamblers. She was looking for the soldiers she had earlier lured into a hand of Poker, offering a complimentary round of whiskey and the promise of a free dance at the game's conclusion, win or lose.

She spotted Charles Cora, the most handsome and well dressed man in the city. He was wearing a Bowler hat and sitting in the corner behind a ridiculous amount of chips. Across from him sat Arabella's soldiers in waiting, backs to her, their shoulders slumped. Fixated on Cora's thick, healthy mustache, she swayed towards the table like a snake, every eye in the house on her as she passed. Charles did not look up. She approached the Calvary men, slid her hands across their backs and asked, "Ready for that dance?" They were. The men had each just lost all of their wages, three entire paychecks, to the dapper Charles Cora. Arabella Ryan took turns spinning around the dance floor, as promised, with the horsemen then the drunk cavalry men stumbled out, their pockets empty.

Belle sat down onto Charles Cora's lap, and took the glass of whiskey out of his hands. She took a sip. Then she took a gulp. Charles pulled her closer to him, her nose, now touching his. Belle whispered, "This seems to be working, Mister Cora." Arabella Ryan and Charles Cora had been successfully running their con for weeks. The serious man revealed a laughing smile under his mustache, showing quite obviously his complete agreement. She draped her arms around him and nuzzled into his neck. In a hushed voice she said, "Working so well, why don't we head west to California, to mine those greedy miners?" Charles' eyes widened. He took the glass back from her and dramatically threw his head back and slammed the remains of whiskey. Slamming the shot glass onto the poker table, he stood, scooping his muse, lover, and business partner up into his arms.

A steamship was leaving that week, and they worked fast to gather a team. The unmarried power couple purchased tickets under the names Charles and Belle Cora. There was little time to waste now that their dream out west had been realized. They boarded the US Mail Company's SS Falcon with their new entourage four days later in the late fall of 1849. The SS Falcon would be the first steamship (with paying passengers onboard) to attempt the potentially fatal shortcut via the Isthmus of Panama.

They would have to cross the jungle on foot and by mule to catch a different ship on the other side to head up to San Francisco. If they survived the expedition, eight thousand miles of travel would be saved by avoiding the voyage around Cape Horn. Comfort and safety were not promised. Always up for a throw of the dice, the group was ready for the challenge.

The rambling passengers on the steamship took turns cheating one another over games of poker as the days of sailing passed. Charles Cora and company had been conning and robbing the well mannered travelers of the assets they intended on bringing into the new world. It wasn't long before Captain Thompson imprisoned Charles in the ship's irons with several of his friends and a few of his newly acquired enemies.

Belle Cora, paid no mind. She took advantage of the time with her rambunctious friends, sixteen year old twin sisters, Charity and Patience. Belle had discovered the sisters in Louisiana and secured them with work at the brothel. The trio had become close, working together for five weeks together before boarding the ship. The twins admired how Belle could so easily separate a man from his dollar. The reason they had jumped at the chance to help Belle and Charles get rich in California.

While the men were locked up below, the three girls kept the other male passengers on the ship company. In the arms of lawyers and politicians, they took s trolls on the deck. They danced with married men who had left their wives at home under the moonlight. Tokens of appreciation showered upon them for the time spent. By the time they had reached their first destination, the three baby faced women had stacked an impressive amount of coin.

After dragging their heavy trunks onto the shores of Panama, the group rolled out their meek bedding on the muddy beach alongside the other travelers from the SS Falcon. Giant bugs swarmed the group, and Charity, terrified of the insects shrieked through the night and kept the team from sleeping soundly. Charles teased Charity, "Toughen up, in the morning, we will forge a giant river, through the jungle, and there will surely be more bugs on the trail."

On narrow boats fighting against the Chagres Rivers current, the tired group had fallen quiet. The boat pushed through the water, traveling less than one mile an hour under the luscious tropical flora and fauna. It did not seem real, as if they were hallucinating, delirious from the tiresome quest. The eyes of submerged crocodiles followed the intruders. Magnificent pumas that perched in the low hanging trees over the shore left their posts and followed the boats along the shore line. Nothing short of intimidating to the usually rough gang.

Belle and the twins passed the time taking turns fanning off the bugs and napping on one another's lap. A native man propelled their boat through the exotic jungle, forcing a long reed pole against the river's bottom, bracing himself against the other end, and walking to the stern as swiftly as he could, over and over again, for seventy-five miles. The girls spent a proper amount of time studying the spectacular muscles of the nude native guide. The sisters and Belle were usually the subject of admiration wherever they went. Hoots, hollers, and demands. What fun to be on the other side.

On the shore, under the stars and among the dense thickets of mangrove trees, the guide roasted the meat of iguana and monkeys. Belle had never seen a monkey until a few mornings prior, and now she was digesting one. It was the last night before the river journey ended, she closed her eyes to sleep and thought of how exotic and interesting it all was. Oh the stories she would have to tell to her new customers in California! She imagined a group of men circled around her in an extravagant parlor, she was telling the story of witnessing pumas and eating monkey meat and the men were losing their minds, clapping and cheering. They hoisted her above their heads, throwing gold nuggets into her lap, and she drifted off to sleep.

As Belle dreamed, Patience's shivering began. She whispered to her sister, "I am so cold". Which seemed absurd in the hot night's air. Charity reached for her twin and found Patiences clothes were soaked with sweat and her skin was burning hot to the touch. Terror stricken, with her hanky, she dabbed the sweat that poured from her twin's face. Waiting in fear for the morning to come.

Belle and Charity attempted to steady themselves in their pompous hats and dresses on top of the old mules as Charles loaded up Patience, who slumped over her mules matted mane. Patience was now far too weak to move, and they would be without fresh water until they reached their destination that evening. The men loaded up the trunks on top of even more of the tired animals. Everyone looked at Patience with sympathy. No one wanted to admit they feared her impending fate on this disease ridden journey.

Prepared for a grueling ride through the jungle of Panama on an exotic beaten path, Charles kissed Belle and saddled up. Charity followed her sister's mule at the back of the pack as they slowly crept into the jungle. Up front, Belle Cora hardly noticed the vibrant flowers and the strange, colorful birds. A rotting scent of death, and failure grew stronger with every passing hour. She could not bear to look back at her ill friend as she held a handkerchief over her face, slowly moving through clouds of flying bugs and the dead bodies of mules and horses that increasingly lined the twenty-five mile leg of the shortcut.

The group arrived in Panama City, dehydrated and covered in insect bites with the hovering possibility of serious illness. A few of the gamblers had become weak with the passing hours. Belle and a distraught Charity went on a search to find help for her sister while the men set up camp. Charles was greeted by a group of travelers he had gambled with on the Falcon who had arrived in Panama earlier that morning. Charles knew one of the men in their group was a doctor. The men told Charles that food sources were scarce for the hundreds of travelers waiting to catch a ride north. Many of the hopeful passengers were now sick with malaria, yellow fever, dysentery or cholera and tragically, one of the canoes on The Chagres had capsized. The doctor had drowned. In the meantime, Belle and Charity searched through the crowd for hours, unable to find help. By morning, Patience was dead.

Travelers had flooded the old city waiting for passage. Some had waited for nearly a month before an approaching vessel was seen beyond the rocky shores. On the streets of Panama, a native woman carved the flesh from a guava with precision. She tossed the chunks next to the slices of freshly skinned pineapple, wrapped them in paper, and handed it to a curious Belle Cora. It would be the first time a Baltimore born woman would taste the strange fruits. She paid the woman and walked back to the camp to share the experience with Charles, and a silent Charity.

Securing a spot on the next ship to California would take a battle of wit, and a handful of cash. Luckily, only a week and a half had passed before Cora's group boarded a side wheeler to California. For the hefty price of one hundred and fifty dollars each. In an act of compassion, Sam, one of Cora's men, had offered to cover Charity's fare, since Charity had yet to speak a word since her twin sister's death.

As they disembarked on the last leg of the voyage, an anxious Charles and grief ridden Arabella stood silently together on the deck of the ship. Hand in hand, they sailed into the magnificent golden sunset. They had survived the jungle, and were at least, healthy, and more than halfway there. Belle and Charles Cora slept the next two weeks away in their stateroom on the ship until they arrived in Acapulco.

At least one hundred soon to be miners from Mexico joined them on board. Life on the ship turned rowdy with the new addition of fresh faces, and the gambling men got back to work. With the help of the Mexican soon to be miners, they learned the game of Monte. It would be nearly two more weeks at sea until they arrived in San Francisco. Just enough time to make another small fortune, if they were lucky.

"I was hanging in a hammock near the bow, alongside a row of bunks, not long after falling asleep I was awakened by a volley of curses and a loud "Get out of here!" More coarse and vile oaths followed and the threat: "If you don't get out, I will cut you down. You are keeping the air from me! I didn't move. One of the men I recognized as Charles Cora, removed a large knife from his pocket. Just then, on the other side of his hammock I saw a pistol gleaming in the moonlight and the man holding it said, "You attempt to cut the

boy down for his purse before me and I will blow a hole through you, you infernal blackleg Southerner. I know you, you used to run a gambling game in New Orleans and you robbed everybody. Get away from that boy! "
-The Journal of Edward L. Williams, December 11, 1849 (en-route to San Francisco via Panama)

The ship sailed along the coast until dusk. It grew thick and foggy and the Captain dropped anchor. Belle Cora looked towards land at the dense forest of hundreds of masts towering over abandoned ships. The ships were packed into the cove like sardines in a tin with no one left to man them. Their crews had by now rushed to the hills.

Rowing to the shore of San Francisco, they passed busy saloons and gambling halls repurposed in the floating ghost ships. Shouting men, working to disassemble the mass of ships that suffocated the bay, hoisted lumber from ship to boat to land. The wood was being carried away to contribute to the city's construction. Development could hardly keep up with the thousands of immigrants arriving each month. A year earlier, Yerba Buena was once the tiny village. Now called San Francisco, the new city had over one hundred thousand men in tents and makeshift shelters.

As the group prepared to disembark, they realized the magnitude of the waiting congregation. In the excitement, Sam hopped off the boat first and disappeared into the crowd with Charity's ticket in his coat. Tensions grew and a commotion on the boat ensued. The purser, fiscally responsible for the collection of the fees for passage roughly grabbed Charity's arm. He demanded that she stay onboard until her ticket was recovered.

A still then silent Charity snapped back, "TIME IS MONEY! You will be held responsible for my damages and losses, plus interest caused by delay of my disembarkment!" The purser and the bold Yankee woman began to quarrel with raised voices. The team, dumbfounded to finally hear their friend speak, stared in awe. The outbreak drew the attention of the waiting group of men, who were anxious to lay their eyes on the sight of a lady. A well dressed man approached the edge of the dock. He tossed a bag of gold at the purser.

Belle, this whole time, overwhelmed and distracted in a romantic moment with Charles, had not been paying attention. She looked up at the group and a

Belle's gold hungry vision was momentarily distracted by the weight of the bag that landed at the Purser's feet. Revealing its contents, the purser released Charity's arm. Gaining focus, Belle locked saddened eyes with Charity as she was escorted off the boat. Her best friend quickly vanished in the cold embrace of her new owner into the sea of men. It had all happened so fast. It was in that moment that Belle realized her own worth in the fast moving world of California.

If you were coming to the gold fields from the North, you were sure to pass through Marysville. The settlement was named after a wife of an employee of the town's founder. The man had struck it rich, and eventually bought half of the territory. His wife's name was Mary Murphy, and she was a survivor of the ill fated Donner Party.

Charles and Belle chose to build in the small mining town and the doors of The New World Gambling Parlor opened in Marysville in 1850. The halls of the entry of the lavish establishment were lined with feverish oil paintings of nude women. Elaborate gold framed mirrors hung in the grand venue. Belle poured drinks and flirted with the customers behind a bar that ran the length of an entire wall, held by intricate brass monuments. Charles played in the hall where gamblers had the decision between poker, roulette, faro or dice.

The Cora's earned a fast profit up until just before it's one year anniversary when the New World Gambling Parlor burned to the ground. Belle and Charles gathered what could be salvaged from the New World Parlor which was nearly nothing. Without worry, the couple looked to start over. In April, Belle and Charles decided to move the operation to the small town of Sonora.

In Sonora, there were at least five thousand people occupying the once Mexican camp. It was now a booming mining town in dire need of entertainment. When Belle took a stroll through her new town, she was impressed with the variety of languages spoken on the streets around her. In open air kitchens, Mexican women were making fabulous money selling tortillas, tamales, produce, and sopas smothered in chile sauce. A pretty, smartly dressed french girl served liquor in every decent place in town. On the corner, a white woman from Curtis Creek offered apple pies for five dollars. This is the equivalent of one hundred and eighty-four dollars in 2022.

The mix of cultures was mesmerizing to Belle. At the end of the street, a large group of men had gathered midtown to bet on bear fights. There was a smartly organized village of Chinese immigrants tents midtown that offered laundry service and opium dens. The Mexican settlers' homes along the street were decorated in romantic fabrics and flags. Dance halls spotted the town, where the men paid in gold dust for the guaranteed close proximity of women. There were bawdy houses in operation, mostly run by Mexican men.

In Sonora, she used the name Arabelle Ryan. She and Charles found and purchased a home they made into a gambling den and brothel near Woods Creek. Belle paid close attention to the design and the comforts offered. It was called "The Sonora Club".

Business boomed when the venue opened in 1851 with Charles dealing card and Belle drawing in the crowds with her sure fire charm. She was the ultimate picture of success. In a short nine months, they accumulated a profit of over one hundred and twenty-six thousand dollars, the equivalent of nearly 4.4 million dollars in 2022. The plan was working. They were ready for the big time. Belle wanted to go where there were an endless amount of potential customers. They decided on wrapping it up in the hills and moving to the city they landed in three years prior, San Francisco.

Hundreds of thousands had now come through the port town and they both felt like it was truly the right place to be. In November of 1852, on DuPont Street, Belle and Charles opened her third parlor house. Belle had a white picket fence built around the front yard. Dream realized.

Belle Cora was the leading den mother in San Francisco and the best dressed woman in the city with the handsome and stylish Charles by her side. The Cora House demanded the highest fees in the industry nationwide. Her customers were the best of the best in society.

As a guest of her establishment, you drank the finest champagne imported from France. At her table, you ate the finest foods, and of course, you enjoyed the company of what many considered, the finest woman in the state. You were to be treated like royalty. Judges, Mayors, Politicians and aldermen from across the country traveled to the city to join in on the fun at The Cora House.

A virgin was not so easy to come by in California. Women in general were few and far between. While golden poppies moved in the breeze, inside The Cora House a hired young girl was upstairs, whispering to a miner who was removing his boots. "Please sir, be ever so gentle with me, I'm all shaky inside." The prospector had just paid three times the going rate of the home for the privilege of deflowering a virgin girl. Outside of the room, ten other miners were peering through peepholes, strategically hidden in the bedroom's walls. Belle had sold admission for five dollars a piece to witness the action. It made for good business.

This particular virgin, Emma, who had somehow kept an innocent and youthful appearance in her line of work, was a tremendous actress. She played nervous and scared, night after night, with much success. Emma was the Official Virgin of Belle's home, and she made a whole ten percent more than the other girls for her talented act.

As if by a curse, just before the one year anniversary of The Cora House, disaster struck again. The Cora House, the three story wooden parlor home had burned to the ground. Just like their first business, The New World Saloon in Marysville.

She was left to start from scratch, yet again. She felt a familiar pain as her heart fell into pieces but Belle chose to show no weakness to her employees and she began delegating the tasks of a new rebuild. She thought of her friend Charity, and the last time she saw her. Time is money.

On the corner of Portsmouth Square there was a newly built two story brick building at Waverly Place and Pike Street. There were other houses of prostitution in the area, including a prominent Chinese establishment across the street. Belle intended to move in, and dominate them all.

She imported furnishings, top of the line liquors, and the finest linens and draperies. Methodist minister Reverend William Taylor had usually been known to attempt to humiliate the local prostitutes. Yet Reverend William Taylor, spoke of Belle Cora's place with high regard. "No residence in San Francisco was more opulent, magnificent without, beautiful within, it was furnished with Brussels velvet, silk and damask. Heavy furniture of rosewood, and walls hung with beautiful paintings, and music from a pianoforte, melodeon, and harp, no house more prominent or beautiful for the situation in the city."

The new Cora House hosted numerous events for the highest class of clientele and Belle's social events were the number one place to be and be seen for the high society. Sins were glorified, even celebrated at the balls thrown in The Cora House. And that was the way these rich white men liked it. The Cora House played an important role in San Francisco, and this put Belle in a place of social and political power. She could whisper in the ear of many legislators in California and they surely enjoyed her sweet voice.

Eventually, a committee was formed to weed out prostitution in San Francisco. The investigation found exactly one hundred houses that were being offered in the surrounding blocks of Broadway, Stockton, Kearney and Clay. Her clientele included some of the hired men on the team. In these men's eyes, her immaculate house was different. It was of a better quality. The Cora House was overlooked.

Belle had come far from the girl on the bench. That girl longed for a husband, and longed to be kept. Belle had become quite wealthy on her own. Unmarried. She was proud of this act of independence. If she was married, she would have no legal access to money or property. She would indeed surrender her rights to her husband. The Married Women Act passed when Belle was seven years old but even then women struggled in attempts to be socially and financially independent. It had left a bitter taste in Belle's mouth. Charles again and again proposed to Belle, and each time she denied him. "You can have my money when you're dead."

Charles and Belle's wild lifestyle continued without a hitch for the entirety of the booming years of the rush. The couple continued to gain riches beyond imagination. That was, until hurt feelings triggered a chain of events that would forever change the future for this woman, and in fact, San Francisco.

Excitement brewed in The Cora House as Belle hurried around the home preparing for her biggest party of the season. She lit the candles and chandeliers around the room and looked over her ladies. The gorgeous woman looked perfect. They were wearing gowns, hand selected by Belle, the finest in the city. She thought back to her days lost and destitute, sewing gowns in the brothel in New Orleans, and laughed. A few hours later, at The Cora House, the party was going wild. Over fifty members of high society had swamped the home.

On the other side of town the same evening, US Marshall William Richardson and his wife were hosting their own soiree. The couple sat at a large dinner table where most of the seats were empty. The roasted chicken was drying out, growing colder on the table. Richardson's wife nervously looked to him, and then to his friend Dr Mills. Mills was the only guest in attendance, and he had begun to drink heavily.

Mrs. Richardson sat at her silent dinner table, horrified to realize, no one else would be walking through their door that night. She looked at the many bottles of expensive champagne that were waiting on ice. As the hours crept into the night and no one arrived, she began growing angry. Shelving the unopened bottles hastily, she thought, how could this be? She had been planning this dinner party for weeks.

At the Cora House, Live music shook the walls and the crowd's dancing shook the floors. They sang loudly, spilled the booze and the women were half dressed by the night's end. It was a night that would never be forgotten by the guests of Belle and Charles.

Across town, Dr. Mills, the best friend of the Marshall and a man in the know, pulled Mrs. Richardson aside in the kitchen. He told the anxious woman of the party being thrown at The Cora House. Perhaps, maybe, the guests had instead gone to that party, for a more frivolous night? The god fearing Richardson was so infuriated she became nearly homicidal.

Crying on her front steps. She tossed her champagne glass into the street and drank from the bottle. How dare these upstanding citizens prefer such a disgusting spectacle than her morally sound dinner party? She drank herself into a stupor, murmuring throughout the night to her husband, "That fucking Cora hussy".

The first palace of dramatic art in San Francisco was The New American Theatre, a large brick and wooden building on Sansome, between the streets of California and Sacramento. It held 2000 people. The following Thursday evening after Cora's wild, and Richardson's non-existent parties, The New American Theatre was sold out for the opening night of the show "Nicodemus, An Unfortunate Fisherman". The show starred The Amazing Ravels, the greatest pantomime artist in the world.

All of the town's society was there. Belle and Charles, made their grand entrance under an ornate domed ceiling with a revolving golden sun, stopping to visit with their acquaintances near the grand white pillars in the main parlor. The theatre patrons gathered around to tell each other elaborate stories.

Under the intricate crystal chandeliers that held hundreds of glass pendants, catching the light of scores of oil lamps, Charles led Belle by the hand to a corner. He pressed her up against the velvet draperies that were swinging from the ceiling. Ruffling the curtains that were held in place by the golden beaks of hand carved eagles. Charles Cora kissed Belle, the love of his life. Everything was perfect with her.

As they stole each other's kisses, and sheepishly gazed into one another's eyes, US Marshall Richardson with his wife and her friend entered the New American theatre. They crossed the main parlor and made their way to the balcony that held the most expensive seats in the house. The large orchestra pit held lower priced seats. Behind it, was a box, draped with velvet curtains. There, the female guests who in society's eyes, were not proper ladies, were placed. The high society flocked to the first balcony, with even more seating found in the higher balconies above that.

The audience was notified that the show was about to begin. Charles and Belle made their way back to the bar for one more round of whiskey, asking to be escorted to where they would be sitting. An usher led the love struck couple away and opened the curtain to the first balcony, where Charles was told it would be the best view for his beloved lady. As they made their way to their seats, a few nosey men in the orchestra pit had noticed Belle, and began to make a commotion. Soon, nearly everyone on the floor beneath them was looking up at her, smiling and winking.

Sitting in front of Belle and Charles, was the US Marshall with his wife, Mrs. Richardson and her friend. The Richardson's had not realized the Cora's had entered the box. The two women were now peering into the crowd full of men, looking up at the balcony. The ladies sat pink cheeked, grinning from ear to ear at each other. It was unusual for the Marshall's wife to draw such attention. She was clearly eating it up. Her friend was massively impressed with the admiring gazes. It soothed Mrs. Richardson's recently bruised ego until, she realized, they were in fact not in awe of her, but that fucking Cora hussy, who was sitting behind her.

Mrs. Richardson, shaking, leaned over and whispered in the Marshalls ear. The hair stood on the back of his neck as he then turned around to look up at the Cora's. He was steaming. His wife had been scandalized by this criminal couple, once again. He stood up, and stormed out of the box to find the manager of the New American theater. The show had begun before Richardson had found the man in charge.

He demanded the Cora's be thrown out of the theatre, or at least be sat in the pit with the scummier patrons of the town. He screamed furiously, as the manager escorted him back to the balcony. The US Marshall made his demands and the manager who still was remaining calm, insisted the Cora's would in fact stay. This handsome couple are regular patrons of the arts, he explained, Belle and Cora chuckled in their seats.

The argument grew louder, and soon, the pantomime act was disrupted by the yelling. It had stopped completely and the audience's attention was once again on the balcony. The Richardsons were then escorted out of the theatre with their humiliated friend. As they were pushed out, the US Marshall hurled a nasty insult at Belle Cora, who softly hushed the man with her dainty finger, then turned back to the audience and gave them a wink.

Two days had gone by, and Richardson and his wife were sitting at home, still in shame. No. Boiling. They had not shown their face outside of the house since the evening at The New American Theatre. Mrs. Richardson was also devastated that she and her friend were not even able to see the performance of Nicodemus. That fucking Cora Hussy.

William gathered the courage to go for a walk. He needed to finally get some fresh air. As he strolled down Montgomery Street, he noticed a little too late that a drunk Charles Cora was walking in his direction. As the men passed each other, Charles locked eyes with Richardson, and before he could look away, Cora blurted out, "Ma'am, your pussy is showing." Richardson, being out of practice after sitting at home in silence with his wife, was dumbfounded. He was unable to come up with a comeback, nothing came out of his mouth, he did not even slow his pace. Charles continued on his way. He won, that time. The Marshall began to walk faster. He tried to think of a good comeback as he headed back home to get himself ready for the long night.

At the Cosmopolitan Saloon, Dr. Mills was surprisingly playing a game of backgammon with Charles Cora. Richardson entered, and saw his best friend sitting with his new enemy. Pushing his way to the bar, he ordered a bottle of champagne. He uncorked the bottle and approached his friend. Dr. Mills, who did not like to see a quarrel, officially introduced the two men. Cora and Richardson reluctantly shook hands and together, downed the entire bottle of champagne, and then some.

Drunk, the two men then went for a walk in the foggy sea air. What started as a friendly conversation, turned into a wave of derogatory comments from Richardson. Charles stopped and turned to the Marshall, and once again called him ma'm, and once again told him his pussy was showing. Richardson growled, "Cora, I should slap you in the face" and Charles laughed, and walked back into the saloon.

Richardson hastily followed him back into the bar. Stumbling, he made his way to the center of the room and called everyone's attention. After the men finally looked his way, he made an announcement to the crowds of drunken men. "Gentlemen, I have just promised to slap Charles Cora in the face, and now I shall do it in front of all of you fucks." The men in the bar pulled William out of the bar and walked him home for the evening.

Richardson was tired of being publicly humiliated by the Catholic Italian man. He sought to finish the feud once and for all. The next morning he paced up and down Montgomery, hoping to run into Charles Cora. From gambling hall to gambling hall, he roamed for hours into the late afternoon, promising revenge on Cora to all who crossed his path.

The Marshall was walking down Kearney Street and when he made a turn onto Clay, he finally saw Charles Cora. Cora was walking towards him with Ragsdale, a mutual friend. Cora reached out to William to shake his hand and once again, the men shook on it, and went in for a drink to seal the deal. Inside of Hayes Saloon the two men made a toast to new beginnings. They drank there for a few hours, and later made their way back to the Cosmopolitan for another bottle of Champagne, then parting ways.

Later that night, Charles was gambling in the Blue Wing Saloon when a man who he had recognized, but did not know, told him he had a friend who was waiting outside who wanted to talk to him. Charles made his way outside, and never returned.

Back at The Cora House, Belle watched for Charles all evening and had given up on the idea of waiting for him any longer. She turned down the lamps. Lonely, Belle couldn't sleep. She paced the building from room to room, making sure the doors were left unlocked, she was getting worried about Charles. She did not know that a few streets away, he was in big, big trouble.

William Richardson was the "friend" in question waiting outside of the bar for Charles Cora that night. The two men walked together toward the waterfront of San Francisco into the brisk fall air. As they approached the corner of Leidesdorff Street, Charles and Richardson began what became a heated verbal exchange. In the height of the argument, Richardson pulled out two hand guns, and Charles Cora swiftly knocked both of them out of his hands and shot the US Marshall, William Richardson in the head with his derringer, killing him instantly. The fire bell rang out loud and clear from the Big Six Engine House and the sleeping town woke at the call for the city's Vigilante Committee. Charles Cora had quickly been arrested, and the crowd began to form.

In the morning, an eagle circled the majority of the population of San Francisco, who had now gathered in front of the nearby Oriental Hotel. It seemed as if it knew a riot was about to ensue. Word had traveled to Belle and she was rushing around the Cora House like a mad woman, from room to room, this time excusing all of her girls from their posts and hurrying them out the door. She almost paused as she noticed an eagle flying away from the crowd, but instead slammed the window shut with haste.

Sam Brannan, the most famous man in San Francisco, soon appeared in front of the masses. He gave a passionate speech, throwing his arms around wildly to the growing crowd. Brannan said the people needed to make up for the failure of law and order in California. The crowd cheered. As his voice raised, the city got louder.

Sam Brannon demanded that lynch law must take over. The civil authorities quickly arrested the protesting Brannan and pushed him down the street into the jailhouse. Sam was a massively wealthy and connected man and was able to post bail right away. Once released, he wasted no time, and quickly returned to the crowd. He had another fiery speech prepared and he was warmly welcomed back by the growing mob who desired revenge for the murderer of the US Marshall.

Like a restless wave, the mass of people roared all the way from the jail on Broadway at Romolo Place, to the Marshall's personal office in the Merchant Exchange building, where William Richardson's dead body was being held. After a short investigation by the Coroner's jury, it was found that William Richardson had indeed come to his death by pistol shot that was fired by the hand of one Charles Cora.

Belle sat at her desk inside of The Cora House, working tirelessly to secure a strong defense for her partner, Charles Cora. Against this furious mob, it would take a genius to get Charles off the hook. She took a break to pick up the morning's paper, which read, "The harlot who instigated the murder of Richardson and others of her kind are allowed to visit the theatre and seat themselves side by side with the wives and daughters of our citizens."

She used her connections to pull string after string, making arrangements to attain the most expensive attorney in the city. The man she chose was Colonel D.D. Baker, the greatest criminal lawyer in the state. Baker was a convincing public speaker and he demanded thirty-thousand dollars up front to take the highly publicized case. Belle was able to persuade him to only take half of it first, fifteen thousand dollars, as a down payment. She laid the fee down in front of him in gold. Baker agreed.

It did not take much time at all for the angry townspeople of San Francisco to turn against Baker. They were mobbing his front door and degrading him in the streets. He arrived unannounced at The Cora house and tried to return Belle's down payment, and quit. Belle Cora refused to accept the man's offer to return the gold. She used her charms to persuade the frightened attorney to continue defending Charles in what the newspapers were now calling The Cora Case. For the next two months, Baker worked to prepare for the trial of his career. No one would see Belle again until Charles Cora's day in court.

It was foggy the morning of January 17, 1856, the day the contentious and highly publicized trial was to finally begin. Belle locked the doors of The Cora House behind her and began the solitude walk towards town. Her mind racing with all of the potential outcomes of a decision that would be made today. As she got near, she recognized a bright, familiar face in the crowd. Her heart did a backflip, she couldn't believe it. It was Charity.

Charity was standing at the front door searching the crowd for Belle's face. Belle beelined for the woman, stopping in front of her. Charity's eyes filled with tears, and the women embraced each other. Charity had by now worked off her indentured servitude and had been living in Sacramento. In the hotel where she worked, she had read about the murder and the trial in the newspapers.

Without speaking a word, the two long lost friends walked hand in hand into the courthouse. With Charity by her side, Belle sat down to watch the love of her life on trial. The proceedings that winter morning were short. Eight votes for murder, and four votes for manslaughter. The stern judge announced that the trial would end with a hung jury. Richardson's wife broke down in tears and stumbled out the door. Belle looked across to the man detained at the other side of the room and winked.

Evidence had been presented that in fact proved this verdict was made in fear of the feisty mob. Rumors began to spread that some of the jurors were bribed by Belle Cora. They were. The judge decided to set a date for a new trial. It would be held in the spring of that year. The public was starting to believe Charles Cora would end up receiving the lesser charge of manslaughter, or an acquittal.

Belle Cora by now had shut the doors permanently to The Cora House. She spent the days waiting for Charles'trial with only her friend Charity to keep her company. The woman passed the time catching up on the years that they had spent apart. They recalled their adventures in New Orleans and then their personal journeys in California and last, the tragedy in Panama. The two women shed many tears for Patience. If only she could be with them now. Belle continued to apologize profusely for letting that man take Charity away that day. Charity admitted the resentment that she had indeed held onto for years, until she saw that Belle was in trouble. They sewed, and sat and waited for Belle Cora to learn Charles' fate.

In addition to the Cora Case, another legal hurricane was brewing. Tensions were rising in the media in California, in-regards to the state seceding with the South and remaining with the Union. The people were divided.

James King of William, the popular newsman published an exposing editorial on the criminal past of James Casey. Casey was a radical editor who favored the South. Casey had recently been released from Sing Sing after serving an eighteen month sentence. Casey had become irate with the doxxing by King.

Less than a block from where Cora murdered Richardson, Casey approached King, flinging aside his short cloak and pulling out a pistol he pointed to his chest. Casey killed King, in a rage of retaliation. Once again, the bell cried out from the Big Six Engine House. What now?

The people of the city were mob crazed. That night in the jailhouse, the two men, Charles Cora and James Casey sat on the dusty floor. The men sat in silence and without eye contact through most of the night. Until James, finally catching Cora's eye, offered out his hand. Cora did not look up. He shook his head.

K"eep your hands to yourself, you motherfucker, you have surely hung us both."

Give us Lynch Law! Tens of thousands of people marched the streets of the large port city, shouting for justice. The scene was out of control. James Van Ness, the city Mayor who had been in office for one year, appeared before the upset people. Van Ness begged the crowd to allow the law to hand out justice. Vainly, a battalion of Cavalry men rode through the crowd. The men, on horseback, attempted to break the mob up, with no success. Soon, the council chambers of city hall were entirely seized by the angry mob.

Belle and Charity sat in the second story window of The Cora House on Waverly, watching the crowd pass by in a rage. The front of her establishment had been trashed. Charity had moved in with Belle, grateful to be near her dear friend again. Neither woman had another friendship comparable to what they had built. Belle was also the only woman in California that had known Patience, and that made them feel that much closer. Although Charity was always just one room away, her friend was growing more depressed by the day. Belle had found her way back to the loneliness she had learned when she first left her family home in Baltimore. The two women lived under one roof, in a familiar silence.

Over the previous week, over six thousand members had traveled to join the forces of the Vigilance Committee. The men had arrived bearing shotguns, muskets and knives, and brass cannons. The murder of James King of William had sent the population over the edge. They would not settle down until they saw blood. Organized into twenty-five groups of one hundred, the armed citizens made camp overnight, clearly ready for battle. They had demands and the committee insisted they get the right to run their own lawsuit, trial, and arrests.

Thousands of blood thirsty men crowded around the jailhouse on Broadway on the 18th of May to challenge the authorities. They demanded Charles Cora and James Casey to be released to the mob, who felt the men deserved to face a trial held by the People. When the Sheriff refused, a loaded cannon was rolled out from behind the crowd. Men shouted and laughed as it was wheeled around and was then directed right at the jail house's locked door. Again, they demanded the men were handed over. The time the Sheriff changed his mind and struck a deal with the vigilantes.

Two days later, Charles Cora and James Casey stood trial by the Committee. They had defense and were given the chance to speak for themselves. However, the attempts were not enough to save the men. That afternoon, it was decided that both men were to be hung, two days from then. At the headquarters on 41 Sacramento St. at Fort Gunnybags, just off Battery.

Three thousand militia men had lined the walls he morning of the day Charles and James were to be hanged. Belle arrived at the holding cell in her finest gown, styled to the nines. She negotiated with the leaders of the committee. "Could you find it in your heart, sir, to please, please allow me to stay in the cell with my lover, for the final hours of his life?" Belle's dramatic personality awarded her the time with Charles.

In another act of Belle Cora's uncommon self-rule, Belle told Charles she was ready to be his wife. They were married in the cell right then and there. This final sneaky move of Belle would set her up to inherit his entire fortune. For the first time legally, Belle officially took Charles last name, just one hour before he was to be executed.

The church bells rang out for the funeral of James King of William at 1:21 pm. When the bells stopped ringing, James and Charles were hung side by side from the second story windows of Fort Gunnybags.

The death of Charles Cora symbolized the city's changing values. It would be the end of an era. The mark of the true end of what would be known as the lawless days of The Gold Rush in San Francisco. The days crimes went unanswered, were over.

After the conviction, Belle secluded herself for an entire month. Charity, eventually feeling unwelcome, quietly packed her bags and left the house without a goodbye. Belle Cora returned to the public a week after she left, looking different. Belle sold the Cora House, and donated the remains of her enormous riches to charity, and vanished.

Belle Cora died of pneumonia on February 17, 1862. You can visit her grave in San Francisco in the Cemetery at Mission Dolores. You will find her there, resting peacefully for eternity, next to Charles Cora, the man of her dreams.

Assassination of James King, of William, corner of Montgomery and Washington Streets, San Francisco, California / / Richardson=Cox, sc.Execution of James P. Casey and Charles Cora in front of the vigilance committee rooms, San Francisco, California. San Francisco California, 1856. Photograph. https://www.loc.gov/item/91732249/

9

Two American men were visiting China in the early 1850s. They stopped to make a note in their journal. "Between the graves and the city wall stood a low building, in a clump of cedar trees. That is the Baby-tower, tended by the Buddhist Nunneries. The top, which rose about ten feet above the ground, was roofed, and looking into it, we saw that the tower was filled. In a mound of bamboo straw that moves with the crawling of the worms, tiny legs and arms, and little fleshless bones, protrude. Was this a cemetery or a slaughterhouse?"

The Chinese said it was only a tomb. The building was one of many commonly built structures for the disposal of infants. It would be used by parents too poor for burial costs or to ashamed of killing their child. There was no inquiry, no check. The parent had the power to kill or to save.

The infant would be tied up in a package and thrown into one of the openings of the tower. Those who passed by had to ignore the screaming cries. The babies left in the towers soon died of hunger, cold, or the heat but sometimes survived for up to two days until whoever built the tower would clear it out and either bury the babies or burn the heap. They would spread the ashes over the land. Female gendercide, also known as genocide, and infanticide, has been practiced since ancient times to avoid poverty, and for population control.

Buddhists condemned the killings of young girls and insisted it would bring bad karma. However, the Buddhist belief in reincarnation meant that they believed that the death of an infant was not final. The child would be reborn. This belief eased guilty feelings that consumed parents.

Many families were struggling to feed all of the members just to survive in 19th century China. Confucianism in China considered a son necessary for the guarantee of provision of security. The pressure on a woman to have a boy, and not have more than one child was colossal. If you were a woman born in China at the time, you would not have been considered as valuable in comparison to being born male. You would have been extremely vulnerable to being given up, killed, or sold off by your family. If not, you would have been perceived as subservient, your future role, a homemaker. It was believed that money spent on raising a female was not a logical investment.

If your family was not in danger of poverty, actions would be taken to make you a more desirable bride. In China the desirable women bore a three-inch foot, known as a *golden lotus*. Four-inch feet or *silver lotus*, were considered respectable, but feet that were five inches or longer were called the *iron lotus* and much less desirable. The prospects for marriage would be low for a girl with the iron lotus. Tiny feet were made possible by the process of foot binding, which began when a girl was five or six years old. The pain was excruciating, yet millions of Chinese women were devoted to the tradition.

Try to imagine enduring the process as a young child. First, your toenails would be cut down as short as possible before submerged into extremely hot water. Your feet were oiled and as you were massaged, all of your toes, except the big toes, were snapped and forced flat against your sole, making a triangle. Bent double, the arch of your foot would be strained and folded in half. Ten feet of wide silk strips would have been used to bind your feet into place. Your feet wood bleed and ooze pus. They would be remove and replace the silk every few days to avoid infection, but the extra hanging flesh would be left to rot or cut away.

Next, you would be forced to walk long distances to hurry the breaking of the arches in your feet. The silk wrappings would get tighter and tighter and your heels and soles would smashed together. This process would last for two years and when finished, there would be a cleft in your foot so deep, you could hold a coin in it. Foot binding goes as far back as the 11th century. Clearly social forces in China had long suppressed women.

Afong Moy was the first Chinese female was brought to the United States, soon after the first Chinese sailors and peddlers visited New York in the early 1830s. Two men took her from her home to New York City, banking on exhibiting her as "the Chinese Lady".

It would be another ten years before the United States and China signed a treaty of peace, amity, and commerce, and another three years before three more Chinese Immigrants arrived on the East Coast for schooling.

In 1848, the first Chinese woman arrived in California. Marie Seise had worked as a longtime housekeeper for the English couple that brought her from Hong Kong. The Captain and his crew of Chinese men of the Ship who brought her, had deserted the vessel upon arrival in San Francisco. He founded a town in the foothills of the Sierra Nevadas, which was named Chinese Camp. By 1849, Marie and fifty-four Chinese men were living in California.

Soon, the news of gold for the taking spread all the way across the ocean and arrived in Hong Kong and the Chinese provinces. They were literally told California was a single mountain made of gold nuggets. They called California Gum Shan (Mountain of Gold). Posters, maps and pamphlets with exaggerated accounts of the golden hills of California were distributed at all the Chinese ports, and the news traveled inland. The Masters of the Vessels quickly became wealthy with the passage money. It was not long before 20,000 Chinese Men were sailing to Gum Shan.

Exploitation

10

From Hong Kong, a clipper ship was slowly making her way to California. Many long weeks had come and gone on an endless rocking sea, and the voyage would soon be nearing her midway point. On the dock, a tall, young slender Hakku woman stood with broad shoulders facing the sea. She gazed out into the restless black waves that lit up under the magnificent moon. It was late and the rest of the Chinese passengers had bedded down for the evening in steerage where the food was stored. She was the only Chinese woman on the ship. The sea foamed, the wind brushed her rice powdered skin. She was all alone now.

The woman's opium addicted father had sold her for a low price to a Tong member. He would to sell her to the high man in California as a slave. The Tong man labeled her as his wife when she boarded the clipper ship and told her not to speak to anyone on board. She did what she was told. Until he became sick, and died on the ship. For the first time in the woman's life, she was free and anything was possible.

The woman, whose name was Ah Toy, contemplated what life would have been like to arrive in a foreign land, the property of a stranger. She would be the second Chinese woman to arrive in California. There would be so many men, with pockets full of gold. A smirk attempted to escape her thin pink lips. She was sailing to a new life. In a frosty breath, she let out a whispered cry of relief. Ziyou. Freedom.

Ah Toy felt the presence of someone step behind her. Two strong hands settled on her hips and began to caress her lower back. She let out a dramatic sigh. She felt a kiss on her neck and the nudge of a hat pressed against the back of her head. She swallowed the smirk and turned around to look into the adoring eyes of the Captain of the ship.

After her owner's death, it was not comfortable in steerage for Ah Toy, the only woman on the ship. It hadn't taken long for the Captain of the Ship to recognize the beauty in the only Chinese woman on board, who he met when her "husband" had died on the passage. The Captain, a sensitive man, took a liking to the woman. Within days he had taken her in, giving her his bed to sleep in, food to eat, and tea to drink.

Ah Toy was either too afraid or too smart to let him know she was merely a slave girl, and not the wife of the dead Chinese merchant. She allowed him to believe she was deeply saddened by his passing. The more helpless she seemed, the more the captain doted on her. In the evenings, Ah Toy indulged the Captain, offering her delicate body to the tall, American man. He had never seen a Chinese woman naked and embarrassedly admitted that he had believed what was under the clothes of the Chinese woman, was not entirely the same as a white woman. He told her, any white man in California would be curious about her body and would pay a good deal of money to let him have a *look-see*.

In gratitude for her affections, he showered his new mistress with gold and gifts, night after night, amounting to a small fortune. The Captain spent his down time teaching her how to communicate in English. Preparing the helpless, lonely woman for what he assumed would be misery upon her arrival in California.

The clipper ship touched at the Sandwich Islands. They backed the main yard off of Diamond Head, sent the mail ashore, and picked up one missionary determined to save souls in California. As the ship left the islands, three beautiful Kanuka maidens swam alongside the ship. Their skin glistened with each stroke, their swimming motion mimicked an aquatic dance. Ah Toy wondered if they were mermaids. There would be less than two weeks to go.

Ah Toy lay nude across the bed in the Captain's quarters. Slowly, she sat up and reached for her hot tea, careful not to move too quickly and wake the sleeping man. It had been nearly five weeks since her new freedom had been realized. Ah Toy, clearly a savvy woman, had many weeks to think about her upcoming venture. Tomorrow, she will disembark in California, stepping foot into San Francisco, and into her new life. Rather than being held, Ah Toy was holding. Ziyou. She wrapped her delicate fingers around the cup and sipped it slowly, and whispered a newly learned phrase to the napping Captain who laid at her unbound feet, "You, know nothing".

Norman Assing, stood near the entrance of the wooden building he had made his bakery. In San Francisco, looking out his small, single front window.

The newest ship to arrive had unloaded and men were coming over the hill in droves. With every ship, the town became more interesting. Norman liked to keep eyes on everything.

The excitement on the arriving men's faces brought AsSing the memories of his own sixty-eight day journey from Hong Kong. Norman AsSing was one of the first Chinese men to arrive in San Francisco. He traveled with only three other passengers and a cargo of ordered Chinese goods on the ship, The Swallow. The Chinese men did domesticated work happily, unlike the White men. While gold remained rich for the taking, the Chinese were warmly welcomed. The Chinese decided to form associations for mutual protection, and shortly before Ah Toy's arrival, AsSing, was chosen to be the high man.

He examined the scene in the square, it was absolute chaos. Men were signing up for work, for wagons, and they were ready for a drink. The saloons and restaurants were filled. As AsSing watched the chaos of the newcomers spread through the town, he found himself doing a double take. Has the day come so soon? It could not be.

In the approaching crowd, in a colorful gown under a yellow silk shawl, stood a tall Chinese Woman, right there, in Gum Shan. She was walking alone, and carrying her own trunk. A smile stretched across his face, he moved to open the door and peer out to watch her further. She was beautiful. Norman AsSing decided right then, he would make her his wife.

AsSing knew, a beautiful Chinese wife was all he needed. He was on a mission to become an American millionaire in San Francisco. The woman in the yellow shawl was strong no doubt, for she had survived the journey to California and he was going to need a woman like that. Surely, she would also need him. He watched her enter the saloon across the street. AsSing awkwardly jumped to grab his hat and locked up his bakery, mid morning.

Ah Toy sat across a small wooden table from a pushy Norman AsSing, preparing herself to refuse his offer. AsSing told her that life would be hard for a woman like her. Maybe his first mistake was introducing himself as the high man in California? Or maybe it was assuming she was a helpless woman who would be smart to move in with the stranger? Either way, she was not interested.

Ah Toy could only think that this man was the high man she would have been sold to. She had already found her freedom, and here the high man was, trying to take it away. The audacity! Ah Toy did not let the man finish, instead she stood up mid conversation, pushed her chair in, and looked AsSing dead in the eyes and said, "You know nothing". She left the building. Every man's eyes were on her until the door swung shut, then they all shifted to Norman. He hung his head in embarrassment.

Ah Toy hastily moved up the street, and into another saloon, throwing her trunk down in disgust. She looked to the beautiful French woman who stood behind the bar. They smiled at each other, and the woman slid a glass of whiskey to Ah Toy. "C'est la tournée du patron." Through a mix of broken English, Cantonese and French the story was told, and an arrangement was made.

Thanks to her new friend's connections, a man who was headed to the mines in Chinese Camp let her take over rent in a small residence. The home was right off Portsmouth Square on the alley Clay Street. The Captain's gold paid two months of rent, and afforded her furnishings and rugs for the dirt floors. At the end of the day, Ah Toy shut the door to the crazy world outside that was Gum Shan. Her own place. Ziyou.

Ah Toy had become used to the men in San Francisco staring at her as she went about her morning business while further decorating her room. Ah Toy was appalled and empowered as she smartly navigated her new city. It was upside down compared to home, where Ah Toy had been deemed worthless. In her new home, Ah Toy looked down at her large feet, with confusion. She had spent her entire life as undesirable.

Her feet had been far too big to bind, and Hakka people did not traditionally practice binding. For this reason the Hakka women usually did not move up in social rank. The Golden Lotus, like a small corseted waist for the English, was a representation of the height of female refinement, a symbol of the elite. A Chinese woman's foot size was considered its own form of currency in China, and it was dripping with sexual overtones. The men in San Francisco, however, did not seem to mind her feet, they were no different from any they had seen.

Two weeks later, at least twenty rough looking men lined Clay Street near Portsmouth Square. The men were waiting to see the woman that the newspapers were calling “strangely alluring”. It had not been the first visit for many of the men in the crowd, who were already regulars, although everyone was equally anxious. When it was finally their turn, eight men at a time dropped an ounce of gold each into the deep tin can for a look but ‘do not touch’ show.

The men stood at their chosen peephole, peering into the mysterious woman’s empty room. A few moments later, Ah Toy appeared in a form fitting sheer kimono. As she slowly removed the robe, she would reveal her pearly white naked body, positioning herself on her bed in an alluring pose, exposing herself completely. The men would stamp their dusty boots and howl to the sky. The tin container rattled with every nugget dropped into it. A fee gladly paid. An ounce of gold was worth over eighteen dollars then, the equivalent of two thousand dollars in 2022.

Unlike many of the Chinese men from her homeland that had come as indentured on ships, Ah Toy had no boss. All of the riches that were piling up night after night were hers and hers only. Thanks to a large bag of gold, many weeks of English lessons and a business idea from the Captain of the ship that she had boarded as a slave. Ah Toy was the first Chinese sex worker in San Francisco was quickly the highest paid seductress in the new state. Norman AsSing, was not happy about it.

On a trip to a silk merchant, she had just finished choosing the luxurious fabrics she would purchase to cover her walls when she noticed AsSing enter the establishment. She moved fast to pay the owner of the shop. Ah Toy had since learned that AsSing was the organizer and leader of the local Chinese protection ring, attempting to gain control of the Chinese Community, and become a millionaire. Ah Toy also wanted to become a millionaire, and she wanted to do it on her own, without the high man.

AsSing knew nothing. The merchant added up the cost of the fabrics, and AsSing stepped closely behind Ah Toy who quickly threw more than enough gold on the counter. Examining the gold nuggets, the shop owner told Ah Toy he could not accept the payment, it was brass. Ah Toy was furious. Was this AsSing’s doing? As the merchant accused her of trying to fraud them, she was forced out of the store. She quickly grabbed the unacceptable nuggets and rushed home, humiliated.

At home, Ah Toy shuffled through the tins that held her earnings, and realized many of the nuggets were clearly not gold. They were in fact, brass. The next morning, determined to do something about the problem, she hired a fellow Chinese man to stand at the entrance and weigh out the gold. She would never be taken advantage of again.

Ah Toy stood in front of the judge in an apricot satin jacket with green pantaloons. Her long raven hair was in a gorgeous chignon with black, pencil thin eyebrows drawn onto her white rice-powdered skin. The young woman explained how she had discovered the brass filings, and dumped a china basin that was full of the fake gold onto the table as evidence. The judge asked her what service she provided in order to attain so much gold? The court gasped as Ah Toy told him they came to gaze upon her beauty. He asked her why she came to San Francisco, she replied, "To better my condition". The judge dropped the charges, yet the reporters loved the woman and in the papers, they called out the customers that were in attendance who Ah Toy had suspected of the same fraud. They put their twist on the story, shaming the clients publicly. Ah Toy had become the first Chinese woman to represent herself in court in California.

In 1850, Ah Toy walked towards the water, where the newest ship from China had arrived. She had heard there were five Chinese women at the dock. As she arrived, she saw the smallest of the five women, walking with her trunk, behind AsSing. She picked up her skirt and hurried to the other four ladies and introduced herself to them in their native tongue. Aloy, Asea, Ah Lo and Ah Hone were relieved. Back home in China, sex was not frowned upon in their culture and Aloy and Asea agreed to begin to work for her. Ah Lo and Ah Hone went on to be independent sex workers. One month later, Ah Toy moved the business into a bigger house.

Ah Toy was sound asleep when her home was rushed in the early morning by four men who tied her up and blindfolded her. She had recognized the men, they were members of a Chinese Tong, or gang in San Francisco. The Tong members pushed her over the poppy lined trail and told her that she was being deported. Her passage to China had been arranged.

When the blindfold was removed, Ah Toy found herself sitting in front of AsSing. Of course. She exploded, loosening the ties on her wrist and drew a pistol. AsSing tried to explain she was going back home where she belonged. She forced her way out of the building by gunpoint. She ran straight to the courthouse. The men followed her for a short distance, and reported back to AsSing where she went. He quickly got dressed in his best.

At the courthouse, AsSing explained to the judge that a man in Hong Kong had written, claiming Ah Toy as his wife. Her husband demanded she return home. AsSing asked that the courts stay out of it and let their community handle the matter in its own way. Ah Toy explained to the judge his jealousy of her own success, earned without his assistance, leaving him no cut. AsSing was nothing and he knew nothing. The community was in awe when Ah Toy became the first Chinese woman to win her case on her own.

The following year, AsSing picked up the newspaper, and scoffed at what he read. "Last evening, about eight o'clock, that portion of the city in the vicinity of the Plaza was aroused by a certain nondescript noise… When we arrived near the spot where the outcry was proceeding, we found Ah Toy in full chase after a suspicious looking individual, who had the appearance of being a volunteer to the Indian War. The thief kept ahead for a time, but Ah Toy was too swift for him, she seized him by the collar very much in the style of a police officer, and demanded a diamond pin which he and his party had taken away from her, the pin was valued at three hundred dollars."

AsSing set the paper down. It was taking more than he thought it would to bring this fiery woman down. By then, Ah Toy had gained respect and undeniable success socially, politically and financially. She now ran two boarding houses in a middle class neighborhood at 34 & 56 on Pike Street, as well as two establishments in Stockton and Sacramento. That year, a vigilante crew formed of seven hundred protestant men and their focus quickly turned against sex work and foreigners. As the Frenchman, Mexican and Chileño were driven out, the persecution shifted to the once well received Chinese.

John A. Clark, the brothel investigator, fixed his mustache in the mirror at his home. AsSing had put in many complaints to the Vigilance Committee, who had with his help, just deported Ah Lo, Ah Hone. Clark had been tasked with deporting an uppity woman who had been dragging white men to court. Across town at her Waverly Place House, Ah Toy had been watching out the window as a fancy white woman moved in across the street. A hired man outside was painting a fresh coat on a new white picket fence. Ah Toy saw an eagle soar above as she called out to Aloy, asking her, what is the new neighbor's name? She looked out the window as the woman across the street stepped outside onto her porch. "M'am, Her name is Belle Cora, and she is the most successful madame in the state." Ah Toy cringed.

That was when John Clark showed up at her door. Aloy let him in, and Ah Toy went right to work. She knew exactly who the man was. It did not take long for Ah Toy to seduce Clark, the man who held the fate of her livelihood in his hand. He fell in love with her and they had an affair that lasted over a year, and thanks to her alluring ways with Clark, her businesses were spared.

Ah Toy established herself in the business of importing girls for the local houses of prostitution and her own brothels, before the Tong's fully controlled the "red light district" of San Francisco. There are records of Ah Toy assisting in building the brothel empire, by going to China and purchasing eight women for $40 each and paying $80 per woman's passage. She would sometimes sell the women for over one thousand dollars each to Chinese merchants and gamblers.

When the women arrived in San Francisco, they were kept in an underground cavern called the Queen's Room. In the Queen's Room, the older retired women trained the new girls, some of whom were purported to be as young as eleven years old. Most had believed they had been brought to San Francisco to marry a wealthy husband. She made a number of these trips and had been arrested and convicted several times for keeping a disorderly house, while the white Madam's like her neighbor Belle Cora were not accused of the crime. By the late 1850s there were nearly seven hundred Chinese women in California and nearly six hundred of those women were sex workers. Frank Soule, who was a local literary figure, had by then publicly blamed Ah Toy for the coming of several hundred Chinese prostitutes to SF, under "her advice".

Like I described when we talked about the Cult of True Womanhood, respectability was connected to the purity and moral authority of white women. Many of these sex workers had been tricked, bought or stolen and forced into the trade. White men felt it was acceptable to ignore their religious and moral codes and fulfill their sexual needs with women of different races, who were considered subordinate. Chinese women were stereotyped and singled out for condemnation. This is still happening today and has left a lasting impression that has remained for over a century. In the years following, the anti-Chinese movement ran rampant and there was too much pressure on Ah Toy. She had become a self-sufficient woman in a country that was not her own, in a society where men dominated. She finally withdrew from the business. She sold clams, and lived quietly off her fortune until 1928, when a death announcement of a Mrs. Ah Toy ran in the San Francisco Examiner, within days of her 100th birthday.

Devotion 11

"I thought where he could go I could, and where I went I could take my two little toddling babies. Mother-like, my first thought was of my children. I realized then the task I had undertaken. If I had, I think I would still be in my log cabin in Missouri. But when we talked it all over, it sounded like such a small task to go out to California, and once their fortune, of course, would come to us."

After a time the hard traveling and worse roads told of our failing oxen, and one day my husband said to me, "Unless we can lighten the wagon we shall be obliged to drop out of the train, for the oxen are about to give out." So we looked over our load, and the only things we found we could do without were three sides of bacon and a very dirty calico apron which we laid out by the roadside. We remained all day in camp, and in the meantime I discovered my stock of lard was out. Without telling my husband, who was hard at work mending the wagon, I cut up the bacon, tried out the grease, and had my lard can full again.

The apron I looked at twice and thought it would be of some use yet if clean, and with the aid of the Indian soap-root, growing around the camp, it became quite a respectable addition to my scanty wardrobe. The next day the teams, refreshed by a whole day's rest and good grazing, seemed as well as ever, and my husband told me several times what a "good thing it was we left those things; that the oxen seemed to travel as well again".

Long after we laughed over the remembrance of that day, and his belief that the absence of the three pieces of bacon and the dirty apron could work such a change. It was a hard march over the desert. The men were tired out goading on the poor oxen which seemed ready to drop at every step. They were covered with a thick coating of dust, even to the red tongues which hung from their mouths swollen with thirst and heat.

While we were yet five miles from the Carson River, the miserable beasts seemed to scent the freshness in the air, and they raised their heads and traveled briskly. When only a half mile of distance intervened, every animal seemed spurred by an invisible imp. They broke into a run, a perfect stampede, and refused to be stopped until they had plunged neck deep in the refreshing flood; and when they were unyoked, they snorted, tossed their heads, and rolled over and over in the water in their dumb delight.

It would have been pathetic had it not been so funny, to see those poor, patient, overworked, hard driven beasts, after a journey of two thousand miles, raise heads and tails and gallop at full speed, an emigrant wagon with flapping sides jolting at their heels. At last we were near our journey's end. We had reached the summit of the Sierra, and had begun the tedious journey down the mountain side. A more cheerful look came to every face; every step lightened; every heart beat with new 9 aspirations. Already we began to forget the trials and hardships of the past, and to look forward with renewed hope to the future. The first man we met was about fifty miles above Sacramento.

He had ridden on ahead, bought a fresh horse and some new clothes, and was coming back to meet his train. The sight of his white shirt, the first I had seen for four long months, revived in me the languishing spark of womanly vanity; and when he rode up to the wagon where I was standing, I felt embarrassed, drew down my ragged sun-bonnet over my sunburned face, and shrank from observation.

My skirts were worn off in rags above my ankles; my sleeves hung in tatters above my elbows; my hands brown and hard, were gloveless; around my neck was tied a cotton square, torn from a discarded dress; the soles of my leather shoes had long ago parted company with the uppers; and my husband, children and all the camp, were habited like myself in rags. We slept on the mattress lying on the floor of the wagon. Nothing but the actual experience will give one an idea of the plodding, unvarying monotony, the vexations, the exhaustive energy, the throbs of hope, the depths of despair, through which we lived."

\- Luzena Wilson

It was almost dusk as Luzena Wilson, a Quaker woman wrote in her diary. Her, her husband Mason, her two boys, her brothers and their wives had left with a train of five wagons in May on her thirtieth birthday. Their one-room log home remained back home in Missouri. In it, stayed most of their belongings with the exception of two Bibles, two quilts, one dress, a bonnet, a pair of shoes, and a few pieces of china that she packed away in their prairie schooner. Possessions that would soon mostly be lost or left behind on the trail to California. A trail that was already littered with household items and shallow graves while a steady stream of 49ers and their thin, thirsty livestock traveled across the country at two miles an hour, slower than the speed of the spreading cholera. They will arrive in Sacramento tomorrow.

Luzena got to building her campfire to prepare supper for her famished family surrounded by the twinkling camp fires of the travelers. The flames illuminated canvas tents in the distance. Everywhere Luzena looked, men were laughing and passing whiskey, playing cards or rolled up in blankets sleeping, exhausted from months of travel. As she prodded the fire and prepared her dough, she wished the men would share just a sip of their whiskey, for the Wilson's had long been out. She thought of their arrival the next day in Sacramento, hopefully Mason could find gold quickly, for they would soon be out of supplies and money.

From the shadows, a hungry miner approached her. "I'll give you five dollars, ma'am, for them biscuit." She scoffed at him until she read his face, he was as serious as a heart attack. Luzena hesitated at such a remarkable proposition, five dollars was over two weeks of a man's wage back at home. One hundred and seventy-six dollars in 2021. For a biscuit! "I'll give you five dollars, ma'am, for them biscuit, and ten dollars for bread made by a woman." He pressed a rather impressive shining gold piece into her hand. Eureka! She stowed the gold away in a little black box to later surprise Mason with.

Later that night, as Luzena slept, she dreamt of thousands of bearded miners, striking gold from the earth with every blow of the pick. A part of each of those nuggets, then delivered to her. As Luzena and her family rode to a new camp the next morning, she fantasized about her dream the night before. When they settled in, she went to retrieve the gold she had earned the night before, eager to restock supplies at Sutter's Fort. The little black box she had stored the nugget was gone. It had rolled out of the bottom of the wagon, the contents somewhere on the dusty trail behind them, left with the golden poppies. That night, Luzena wrote in her diary, The nest egg was gone, but the homely bird which laid it, the power and will to work, was still there.

Mason Wilson kneeled at the bed of the American River, his corked glass vial holding only a small amount of gold dust. Filthy, he dug, picked, and shook the dirt from the daybreak until it was too dark to see a difference between the rocks in his pan. Defeated, he slowly walked home after four days and nights upriver, empty handed. How would he explain his immediate failure to Luzena? It had taken them five months to get to California, and they gave up everything to chase this dream of his. Luzena most likely had run out of the remaining supplies, and he was in fear of the outcome of leaving her to manage the camp and their rowdy, young boys all by herself.

When Mason finally reached just outside of his camp he approached he heard a commotion near his canvas tent. His pace quickened and he reached for his knife, ready to defend whatever drunks which were surely making the noise, and most likely harassing his bride. He turned the corner from behind their covered wagon and was astonished at what he saw taking place. He stopped dead in his tracks. Near two campfires, at a row of plank tables that had not been there when he departed, sat twenty dining miners. The men were rowdy all right, whooping and hollering for the good food and for the entertaining jig his sons danced for the tired 49ers, reviving the men's aching souls.

Mason spotted his wife, across the furthest fire, pouring hot coffee into an elderly Chilean man's tin cup. She looked up and saw her husband gazing towards her in disbelief, their eyes locking. She was the most beautiful thing he had ever seen, and what a fool he had been to not see her own potential outside of their marriage and home. The shame in the realization gutted him. As they laid in bed that night, Luzena told Mason that that had been the third seating of men that came for dinner that evening. Each man paid one whole dollar for the meal and she expected them all to return for breakfast, and dinner tomorrow, and the days that followed. Pay dirt.

Mason had been worrying for no reason. The morning before, Luzena had sold off the remaining oxen from the journey, bought supplies from the successful Sam Brannan's store in New Helvetia and bought a stake in a small hotel business. While Mason was panning the river, Luzena was hard at work with her own pan, over a fire, preparing a meal to feed an army. Nearly twice as many dirt covered men lined up outside of Wilson's hotel the next morning.

Word traveled fast, there was an American woman with domestic skills in Sacramento. Unheard of. Dropping the dough into a sizzling pan, she took one moment to take a breath, tilted her head back to kiss the sky, sun beams warming her face. The flap of a bird's wings caused her to open her eyes. Settling into a tree above her gaze was the majestic, fully grown bald eagle who had visited her each day since the Wilson family's arrival. The Bald Eagle and Luzena acknowledged each other. "All the places you could go, and you just want to watch me make biscuits?" She stared up into the tree. Did that bird just nod at her?

In Sacramento, Customers were happy to pay the high price tag for a meal prepared by Luzena Wilson, for the white woman, was a rarity. In 1850, women made up just three percent of the non-Native American population in California's mining region, numbering about eight hundred in a sea of thirty-thousand men. As a married American woman, Luzena Wilson reminded many of the American men of home, of their wives, mothers or sisters. They treated Luzena, as she put it, like a queen. Serving up to two hundred boarders a week and charging each twenty-five dollars, her success afforded the establishment a true building with a roof, more tables and employees. Sourcing the ingredients remained the largest challenge for Luzena in the beginning.

"My first purchase was a quart of molasses for a dollar, and a slice of salt pork as large as my hand, for the same price. That pork was an experience. When it went into the pan it was as innocent looking pork as I ever saw, but no sooner did it touch the fire did it prance, it sizzled and frothed over the pan, sputtered, crackled, and acted as if possessed. When finally it subsided, there was a shaving the size of a dollar left, the pork had vanished into smoke. I found after that many of our purchases were deceptive, for the long trip around the Horn, was not calculated to improve an article which was probably inferior in quality when it left New York. The flour we used was often soured and from a single sieve-full I sifted out at one time a handful of long black worms. The butter was brown from age and had spent a year on the way out to California. I once endeavored to freshen some of this butter by washing it first in chloride of lyme, and afterwards churning it with fresh milk. I improved it in a measure, for it became white, but still it retained its strength. It was, however, such a superior item to the original Boston butter, that my boarders ate it as a luxury. Strange to say, in a country overrun with cattle as California was in the early days, fresh milk and butter were unheard of, and I sold what little milk was left from my children's meals for the enormous price of a dollar a pint."*

-Luzena Wilson

Six months had passed in Sacramento, and during that half of a year, Luzena had crossed paths with only two other white women. Her business had been established and now she longed for a friend. One evening, Luzena put her boys to bed, and under dim light, she wrote out her list of goods needed for the next week. She would make her largest purchase yet in the morning. She set down her steel dip-pen, blew out the beeswax candle next to it, and laid down beside Mason. The rain began to furiously pound on the family home's weak roof, and it did not stop all night.

Days and nights of non stop heavy rain had passed. Luzena was standing over her stove one afternoon, Wilson was preparing supper for the masses when she heard someone yell from outside "the levee's *broke!*" Dropping the ladle onto the floor, she grabbed her skirt, and yelled for the children, running toward the stairs. Mason was just ahead of her and the children trailed behind as they headed to the top floor of the hotel.

Looking out the window, they saw the water coming, floodwaters lapped outside and downstairs of the hotel, Luzena, Mason and her children sheltered upstairs for seventeen days until the waters subsided. Luzena, who was one of the most prosperous women in the territory, had a business that was ruined. The building, the possessions, and the small fortune of barley Mason had been farming were destroyed. They were broke, and scared of more possible flooding in the long winter in Sacramento. Before the flood, Luzena had heard through her customers that men had begun striking it rich in Nevada City. The nest egg was gone, but the homely bird which laid it, the power and will to work, was still there.

Luzena promised seven hundred dollars to a coach driver and his team to take her two children, her stove, and two sacks of flour to Nevada City. She would pay him for their safe arrival upon her success in the town. She wasted no time, began chopping wood, and drove her stakes into the ground. By the time Mason arrived in Nevada City, Luzena, once again had twenty men eating in her establishment, which she called the El Dorado Hotel. It took six weeks for Luzena to pay back the coach driver his seven hundred dollars.

"We had lived eighteen months in Nevada City when fire cut us adrift again, as water had done in Sacramento. Some careless hand had set fire to a pile of pine shavings lying at the side of a house in the course of construction, and while we slept, unconscious of danger, the flames caught and spread, and in a short half hour the whole town was in a blaze. We were roused from sleep by the cry of "Fire, fire" and the clang of bells. Snatching each garment, we hurried out through blinding smoke and darting flames, not daring even to make an effort to collect our effects. There were no means for stopping such a conflagration. Bells clanged and gongs sounded, but all to no purpose save to wake the sleeping people, for neither engines nor firemen were at hand. So we stood with bated breath, and watched the fiery monster crush in his great red jaws the homes we had toiled to build."

-Luzena Wilson

The fire in Nevada City burned much of the town to the ground, including Luzena's "El Dorado" and the Wilson's lost everything.

"The remnant of our fortune consisted of five hundred dollars, which my husband had in his pockets and had neglected to put away, and with that sum we were to start again. For months my health had been failing, and when this blow came in the shape of the fire, my strength failed and I fell sick. Some generous man offered us shelter in his cabin on the edge of the woods. For weeks I was a prisoner there, bound in the fetters of fever. When, at last, my returning health and strength permitted it, we decided to move."

-Luzena Wilson

The five days of traveling was easy compared to their trip to California. When the Wilsons arrived at the last range of low foothills, they pitched their tent and settled beneath an oak tree in a little valley called Vaca, eventually becoming the city of Vacaville. Mason set off to cut hay in order to make money to buy land, leaving Luzena on her own. She created a sign with scrap wood and charred embers spelling out "Wilson's Hotel". She made chairs from stumps and started over again. "The nest egg was gone, but the homely bird which laid it, the power and will to work, was still there.

"The accommodations were, perhaps, scanty, but hailed with delight by the traveling public. The boards from the wagon bed made my table, handy stumps and logs made comfortable chairs, and the guest tethered his horse at the distance of a few yards and retired to the other side of the hay-stack to sleep. The next morning he paid me a dollar for his bed and another for his breakfast, touched his sombrero, and with a kind good morning, spurred his horse and rode away, feeling he had not paid too dearly for his entertainment. My husband's ready rifle supplied the table with roast and steak of antelope and elk from the herds which grazed about us, and the hotel under the oak tree prospered."

-Luzena Wilson

The capital of the State was removed to Benicia about the time that we moved to Vaca Valley, and that point being not far distant, we were on the route of constant travel, and among the men who stopped with us often were some who, even then, owned large tracts of land in the country, and many of whom have since become well known to the public, either through political position or great wealth. We residents of Vaca Valley were an amusement-loving people in the early days of the settlement, and every few weeks saw a ball or party given, and not seldom the town overflowed for the night with the buxom lads and lassies from thirty miles away.

"The largest room in the town—usually my dining room—was cleared to make room for the dancers, and they danced hard and long until daylight, and often the bright sunlight saw the participants rolling away in spring wagons, or galloping off on horseback to their distant homes. The costumes were, like the gatherings, quite unique; the ladies came in calico dresses and calf boots; a ribbon was unusual, and their principal ornaments were good health and good nature; the gentlemen came ungloved, and sometimes coatless. But the fun was genuine, and when the last dance was turned off by the sleepy fiddler who kept time with his foot, it was with a sigh of genuine regret that the many dancers said good morning."

-Luzena Wilson

Luzena, known as one of Vacaville's earliest settlers, invested in properties around the area as the town grew and grew. Mason Wilson had struggled with Luzena's success for a long while and in 1872, he abandoned his family out of the blue and moved to Texas. Luzena lived in Vacaville until 1877, fire once again destroyed what she owned. She moved into a hotel in San Francisco and she spent the rest of her life there, living off real estate transactions.

"The years have been full of hardships, but they have brought me many friends, and my memory of them is rich with pictures of their kind faces and echoes of their pleasant words. The dear old friends are falling asleep one by one; many of them are already lying quietly at rest under the friendly flower strewn California sod; day by day the circle narrows, and in a few more years there will be none of us left to talk over the "early days".

-Luzena Wilson

Thyroid cancer took Luzena on July 11, 1902, at the Hotel Pleasanton in San Francisco when she was 83 years old. Luzena never gave up. She capitalized on her strengths, and found that in the Old West, most men eventually tired of a woman who knew what they wanted.

12

The former Nevada senator William Sharon sat in his San Francisco courtroom divorce trial, watching his lawyers paint Mary Ellen Pleasant as a sinister crone. Sharon's wife, Sarah Hill was a friend of Mary Ellen Pleasant, and Pleasant was being accused of using dark forces to manipulate her friend into wrongfully seducing Sharon. Legend says that late one dark night, Mary Ellen and Sarah Althea buried the Senator's coat in a cemetery. Pleasant had sprinkled a love potion on his underwear and cast spells that would renew the senator's forgotten love for Hill. In the trial, the newspapers fixated on Mary Ellen's voodoo practice, it was obsessed over and reported on across the nation. Rather than rejecting the rumors that day in court, Mary Ellen encouraged them. One day, she carried a voodoo doll into court, claiming she would use it to bring the Senator to his death, and to his death he went, before the trial was even over. It was deeply rooted that survival meant that you don't tell, that you keep secrets. From the beginning, Mary Ellen had deception, concealment and skullduggery inside her armory.

She arrived alone in San Francisco on April 7, 1852. San Francisco was an unsafe place for a woman to be by herself. There were six men to every woman among the population of forty-thousand with at least seven hundred places to drink and gamble. There were at least five murders every week. Mary Ellen was up to the challenge that stood before her.

In a black dress and matching bonnet she stood on the muddy and smelly Embarcadero in front of the large group of wealthy men who had gathered at the docks awaiting her arrival. These men all wanted the same thing, to gain Mary Ellen as their employee. She had one contingency for the highest bidder, she would not be doing anyone's dishes. As the men bargained, Mary Ellen noticed how many men there were. The need for domestic care and housing was obvious. Their wives were not here. The grown men needed a mother. She looked to the sea just in time to see an eagle dive and snatch a fish from the water. She quickly changed her mind. She announced to the men that she would open her own restaurant, and the first boarding house in San Francisco, and she hoped to see them there.

In the heart of today's Chinatown, Mary Ellen would fill the ice bucket in the parlor, eavesdropping on the men's after dinner chat. Back in her room, she took notes. Her boarding house at 920 Washington Street had become the meeting place of some of the city's most prominent politicians. Senators, the, governor judges and financiers moved in. The Governor took his oath of office in her establishment. Mary Ellen hosted luxurious balls and elegant dinners, and she brought in beautiful, classy women to attend her parties and keep the wealthy men company. At the parties, Mary Ellen poured brandy for guests, she listened to the insider information on stock investments, and gained the insight revealed by powerful men. Mary Ellen had trained the young women in her establishments to do the same. They were told to listen in on the men's business conversations and report back the financial gossip to their boss. Mary Ellen would take notes and use the information gathered in deciding her own investments. Mary Ellen used her money to invest in property, businesses and playing in the stock and money markets. On loaning money at ten percent interest and trading in gold and silver.

"My custom was to deposit silver and draw out gold, by which means I was able to turn my money over rapidly."

Mary Ellen won the trust of the elite. She was making a massive fortune, and her accumulation of wealth allowed her to assist former slaves arriving in San Francisco with job placement. She was determined to make it big and bring her people with her and made it popular for high society to hire black people. She planted maids and servants throughout the prominent homes in San Francisco and procured the men of the house with the services of mistresses. Through her network, Mary Ellen knew the gossip of the cream of the crop and the skeletons in every closet of the city. High Society never understood how. Those in the know, made sure to not antagonize her. You never knew what Mary Ellen might know about you.

Mary Ellen fought for young women under stress, both black and white. She found homes for unwanted babies, got them housing, jobs, loans and their legal charges dropped. All the African Americans knew if they wanted something, they could go to Mary Ellen. She would somehow use her influence to get it. Her kitchen became known as the "Black City Hall". The wealthy men assumed from her light skin that Mary Ellen was white had and her business dealings had been made easier for it. Mary Ellen was, in fact, not white at all. Not one drop.

Born in the South, without a last name, Mary Ellen was a descendent of a long line of Voodoo Queens in Santo Domingo. She remembered her mother with fondness. Both her mother and grand mother were Haitian voodoo priestesses. Six months before Mary Ellen's birth, her mother was captured in one of the Caribbean's oldest cities and brought to the States where she was sold into slavery. Mary Ellen was four years old when she witnessed the murder of her mother at the hand of the overseer at the plantation where her and her mother were both enslaved.

Without another female slave to raise the child, the owner of the plantation eventually decided to send her to New Orleans. Arranging for her to receive an education and to work as a linen worker for his friend Louis Alexander Williams, an importer of silks from the Sandwich Islands. The agreement was that Mary Ellen would serve Williams without pay while her education was attained, and she would be freed upon completion. Years passed and when Williams went into debt, he broke the deal, keeping the money for the schooling and placing seven year old Mary Ellen into nine years of indentured servitude.

Her new owner was an aging Quaker merchant they called Grandma Hussey in Nantucket, MA. Mary Ellen learned about business while working in the Hussey mercantile on Union Street, it was so far the only education she had received. Indentured servants could be of any race, and the light skinned black child was told not to reveal her own. It was a heavy burden for an eleven year old. That was, until the summer she met Mary Hussey's granddaughter Phoebe and her husband Captain Edward Gardner. The couple encouraged Mary Ellen to be proud of her heritage and they introduced her to the ideas of Anti-Slavery.

When Grandma Hussey passed, Mary Ellen was sold to Americus Price, a man in New Orleans. Price placed her in a convent when he was old and it was there that Mary Ellen was finally freed. The first thing she did was make her way to Boston, where she found a position apprenticing as a boot maker. She found a new church and Mary Ellen was hired there as a paid soloist. At service each week, Mary Ellen got to know James W. Smith, a wealthy Cuban-American who owned a plantation in Virginia. He was an abolitionist who would use his wealth to purchase slaves and set them free. Smith, like Mary Ellen, passed for white, which helped him serve the cause with that much more ease.

Mary Ellen was fascinated and quickly married James W. Smith. Well-known abolitionists such as William Lloyd Garrison and Wendell Phillips would frequently meet at the Smith home to discuss all of their ongoing efforts. Together they would do great things. Smith and Mary Ellen smuggled hundreds of slaves to Canada along the Underground Railroad via James Smith's track. The track was made up of a series of homes and volunteers. From Canada, they lead the slaves from Nova Scotia to the Smith plantation in Virginia. There, he would fairly employ the slaves whose freedom he had helped secure.

Suddenly, and without warning, Smith's health took a bad turn. On his deathbed, he told his wife to use his estate, $45,000 in gold, to continue their work for abolition. Mary Ellen told her husband, "You know my cause well, freedom and equality for myself and for my people, my love, I'd rather be a corpse than a coward." Mary Ellen moved back to New Orleans and relied on John J. Pleasant, the foreman of Smith's property as she settled Smith's estate. Back in Virginia, when Smith had died suddenly, some felt that it was by Mary's hand, yet nothing ever came of this accusation. Mary Ellen and Smith's foreman JJ Pleasant were united in the cause to end slavery, and soon united, in other ways. The two married in New Orleans, increasing the suspicion tenfold. News of the Gold Rush in California swept the nation and Pleasant decided to leave New Orleans to scout a safer life for them in the gold rush country. To get there, JJ procured a position as a shipboard cook on the route to San Francisco.

Mary Ellen had met Marie Laveau in the social circles in New Orleans. The social activist and voodoo queen Marie Laveau had been intrigued by Mary Ellen, and invited her to stay with her while JJ was gone and learn the practice of voodoo. The granddaughter of Levaux later told reporters, "She was teaching Mrs. Pleasant Voodoo, so she could use it in some way."

Two months had passed and it was said that the Louisiana planters had been urgently searching for Mary Ellen Pleasant and JJ had by now sent for her and her money from California. Mary Ellen had now found a way to mentor her people. Holding her new secrets, she boarded a steamship in New Orleans and left for San Francisco.

The California's Fugitive Slave Act stated that anyone without freedom papers could be sent into slavery. Mary Ellen did not have such papers when she had first arrived in San Francisco. She used two identities to avoid capture. Mrs. Pleasant was the abolitionist/entrepreneur, and Mrs. Ellen Smith was the white boarding house madame who was serving the wealthiest and most influential men in San Francisco. Either way Mary Ellen was leveraging the secrets of prominent men while procuring jobs and privileges for the black people in San Francisco.

While Mary Ellen was in San Francisco, she stayed in touch with her abolitionists friends, taught herself to read and write, and subscribed to William Lloyd Garrison's newspaper, The Liberator. After hearing the whispers of an uprising back in Harper's Ferry, Mary Ellen wrote a thirty-thousand dollar bank draft for the organizer, John Brown. They would hand deliver it.

Mary Ellen and JJ traveled east, where her old friend Captain Gardner met the couple in Boston. Gardner arranged for the couple to travel to meet John Brown in Ontario. Mary Ellen bought land while in Canada, to house the slaves that John Brown had planned to free. She also provided even more money for arms.

Mary Ellen returned the following fall, and in disguise as a jockey she rode in advance of Brown, alerting the slaves of his coming. It was a risky plan, but Mary would have "rather been a corpse than a coward." Brown, a national figure of the anti-slavery fight had led the raid with twenty-one other men, and was caught and hanged on Dec. 2, 1859 for murder and treason. In his pocket, a note was found that read,

"The ax is laid at the foot of the tree. When the first blow is struck, there will be more money to help." Signed, W.E.P.

The officials believed it was probably written by a wealthy Northerner. Not a single person suspected the note was written by a woman named Mary Ellen Pleasant. She had intentionally written her first initial upside down. Mary Ellen Pleasant, unscathed, returned to California. The Emancipation Proclamation passed in 1863, and two years later, for the first time in 1865, she checked "black" on the census.

Three years later, Mary Ellen got on a streetcar and was clearly told that the company would not accept her, because of the color of her skin. Almost one hundred years before Rosa Parks sat in the front of the bus, Mary Ellen filed a suit against the North Beach and Mission Railroad Company. She won the right for blacks to ride the trolley, leaving lasting effects on legal justice for the Black citizens of San Francisco.

White witnesses spoke in the courtroom on Mary Ellen's behalf. She was unable to testify in court, due to the ban on Black testimony against white persons. She waited outside, a golden poppy in her hair. The witnesses confessed, the conductor had loudly stated the racial policies of the company. This case restated the fact that California had no laws that allowed public carriers, to exclude anyone based on race.

When Mary Ellen first came on the ship from New Orleans to California, on the journey around Cape Horn, a Scotsman named Thomas Bell sat down to introduce himself to Mary Ellen, a beautiful woman, roaming down the hallway. "What have you done to arrange such a high class ticket?" he asked the woman, who was traveling alone. She smirked. The two became fast friends, they were both on their way to San Francisco. Thomas Bell was headed to find fortune, and Mary Ellen was arriving in California with $45,000 in gold.

Thomas Bell had since become a director of the Bank of California. All of these years, without anyone knowing, Mary Ellen had been Bell's closest friend and his undercover financial advisor. To avoid issues with her race and gender, Mary Ellen made her personal investments through Mr. Bell. Her businesses had grown and her investment in quicksilver mining and silver and gold exchanges amassed to now a thirty-million fortune for her and her silent partner. Thirty-million is the equivalent of a four hundred and forty-five million dollar fortune in 2022.

The people in San Francisco whispered that Mary Ellen had been using magic to control Thomas Bell and the 30 room Octavia Street Italianate mansion, known as the Thomas Bell mansion that she had designed, funded, and furnished. When she moved in, so did Teresa, his wife whom Mary Ellen had found for him. It was said that Mary Ellen held hypnotic powers over the ladies in the city and brewed and sold love potions to the wealthy women. For this reason, the odd living arrangement, and rumors of events and underground passages in the home, the Mansion became known as the "house of mystery."The people of San Francisco were quick to accuse Mary Ellen Pleasant of murder through the practice of voodoo when Thomas Bell fell down a staircase and died in 1892. The coroner ruled it an accidental death and no charges were filed. Bell's widow Teresa then collaborated on a full-page smear piece in the San Francisco Chronicle. On the front page, the headline read "The Queen of the Voodoos" and the story revealed Mary Ellen's secret life. The article spilled that, Her" connection with the 'underground railway' was an established fact and that the planters whose slaves she had helped cross the border to the free north demanded her life."

It was one blow after another. She then found out her entire portfolio, including the thirty room mansion she designed and had built, was held only in Bell's name. Teresa was able to then sue Mary Ellen and won control of Mary Ellen's estate. It was easy in a system that was loaded against black women and men in late 19th century San Francisco. Mary Ellen Pleasant was declared bankrupt.

Loyalty was one of the Pleasant's virtues, and it was proven when even though she had nothing, she still refused an offer of fifty-thousand dollars for a tell-all on Bell. After a heated argument with Teresa, Mary Ellen left the Bell Mansion forever.

She once wrote in an unpublished memoir, "I don't want to be carried up to victory on flower beds of ease, I would like to go through the bloody scenes." Mary Ellen died of old age on January 11, 1904, penniless. Her request for the inscription on her gravestone was fulfilled, it reads, "A friend of John Brown". Mary Ellen was a protector of newly freed blacks and was a promoter of the greater rights for the black people of California. In the 1890 census, under profession, Mary Ellen wrote, capitalist.

You can visit Mary Ellen Pleasant Park and stand under the six huge eucalyptus trees that tower above the corner of Octavia and Bush. Mary Ellen planted these herself well over one hundred years ago. This is where the Thomas Bell mansion once stood, before it burned down in 1925. Stand. On the corner, you will find her spirit there. It is said if she likes you, and you will know if she doesn't, you should make a respectful request of the voodoo priestess.

It's telling who gets a legend – and who gets a ghost story.

Temptation

13

In Berlin in 1843, King Friedrich Wilhelm IV indulged in a private dance with his entourage from the Spanish burlesque performer Lola Montez. Cigarette smoke curled around her head as she moved to the music, dripping with eduction. The ruthless showgirl either enchanted or appalled everyone she met.

Montez believed it was her destiny to be royalty, she wanted a castle. The King's brother, Prince Albrecht took the showgirl in as his lover. She eventually tired of the prince. One afternoon, she greatly embarrassed him publicly during a royal picnic in front of the entire court. The humiliated Prince demanded that Montez leave his realm. "That's not such a long trip" she said with sass as she turned dramatically towards her carriage and away she went, headed for Russia.

She was next courted by one of the great magnates of St. Petersburg, a Prince. She was unable to secure a royal marriage with the Russian Prince and moved on to Paris. In Paris, Lola Montez had a fling with the former English Hussar, Francis Leigh. Lola was jealous and ended up running Leigh off with a pistol.

Lola spent a year living the most extravagant high society lifestyle in Paris. Her friends were the most fashionable Bohemians in the city. All of this fun was financed by a collection of wealthy men she had seduced. In just that year, she became the mistress of the author Alexandre Dumas, the famous Hungarian composer Franz Liszt who fell so deeply in love with her he wrote a long piece of classical music about their love. Then she ended the year by marrying Charles Alexandre Dujarier, the part-owner of the French Newspaper, La Presse. Dujarier died in a drunken duel months after her wedding.

After her husband's death, the elderly and proper Lord Momsbury took Lola in. He hosted a benefit concert for her, and connected her with Her Majesty's Theatre in London, where she got a gig. He would fund her travels.

The following year she was called to Prussia to perform a private burlesque routine for the aging King Ludwig I of Bavaria. The King was entranced with her figure and gestured towards her chest. "Nature or art?"

The proud Lola responded by cutting open the front of her dress, exposing nature's endowment.

The King instantly fell in love with Lola Montez. He spoiled her rotten, and made her dream a reality by giving the showgirl her own castle, with a pension. The King named her the Countess Marie von Landsfeld, but privately, he called her Lolita. Karl von Abel, The Minister of State objected to the move, and he was removed from his position.

Lola Montez spoke in favor of anti Catholicism, liberalism and supported attacks on the Jesuits. The radical university students in Bavaria backed up their Countess Landsfeld. Pretty much everyone else refused to acknowledge her as Countess. They found her arrogant and impatient. One general declared, "I've never seen such a demon! She told me that I would see what a spirited woman could accomplish when she set all the levers of intrigue into motion!"

During her time in Bavaria, entire ministries had risen and fallen at the beautiful seductress' doing. On February 7, 1848, thousands gathered and rioted the streets demanding the expulsion of Lola Montez after the people realized er wish to become a naturalized Bavarian subject and be elevated to nobility.

The crowd echoed with the chanting,"Down with the whore". The King gave in to his people. His Lolita had vanished to Switzerland and then to London where her newest conquest British cavalry officer Heald bailed her out of jail and they left for Spain.

In a carriage on a street in Madrid, Lola's put his hand on his wife's knee, in a weak attempt to comfort her. Lola hastily pulled away, turning her body to gaze out at the scenery as they were pulling into Madrid. He had been beyond frustrated and completely done consoling the stubborn woman during the last hours of their journey.

Heald was 20 years old to her 27, and the young man had attracted Montez when he received a large inheritance. It was all a big scandal for his crème de la crème family. The life of royalty and great political influence was now three years behind her, and it was taking some getting used to. Lola looked out the window and asked the driver to stop. He did. She got out, walked of the carriage and stood in the middle of the road. She whispered to herself. "That was then, and this is now."

Standing on that same road in Madrid a decade earlier was a young Irish woman named Eliza Rosanna. Eliza was a well traveled British Army brat and ready to start fresh in Spain. The culture in Spain was brand new to her. Her father's regiment had been posted in India and died of cholera when she was three.

Her stepfather was also in the British Army, stationed in India. Eliza was sent to a boarding school in England and was to return to India when she reached the age of sixteen. When the time came, it had been arranged by her mother and step father for her to marry a wealthy, sixty-four year old judge. She was not happy.

On the passage back to India, Eliza met thirty year old, handsome but ill, Irish Lieutenant Thomas James. James was returning home on sick leave. She nursed James back to health in his cabin on the voyage and during that time, the two fell in love. Eliza and Lieutenant Thomas James eloped and ran to Ireland, escaping her upcoming arranged marriage. James though, was a violent man, living with him in Ireland was torture. In 1839 James needed to rejoin his regimen and the couple returned to India.

In India, her beauty made her the new toast of town. A title previously held by her mother. James did not only continue to be abusive in India, he also proved to be unfaithful. When his affair with the wife of another captain was revealed, Eliza saw it as an easy way out. She decided to leave James and return to Britain.

By the time her ship left the dock, a dashing army officer had already caught her eye. It was George Lennox, the married grandson of the Duke of Richmond. Surrounded by peeping eyes, their affair bloomed, the couple perhaps enjoyed putting on the show. The door of Lennox's cabin had swung open rather too often, revealing him lacing Eliza's corset or sitting on the bed, watching her rolling up her stockings. The Captain was so infuriated that he barred Eliza from George's table.

Once they were in London, Lennox set Eliza up as his mistress in London and introduced her to several other influential men. The news of her affair eventually made its way back to Thomas James and James sued her for divorce. Eliza lost everything in the separation on the grounds of her adultery on a shipboard with another soldier, even though it was James who strayed first. The terms of the divorce prohibited either party to remarry, as long as they were both living. Lennox soon abandoned Eliza and she no longer had means of support, facing the dilemma that many women in that era faced, being virtually unemployable as a governess or a lady's companion.

So, on that dusty street in Madrid, Eliza Rosanna stood in the middle of the street, looking into the window of the establishment where she was to begin studying dance. Mobs of men and horses pulling carts were barely dodging the brave nineteen year old girl.

"That was then, and this is now" she said out loud. Snubbing a cigar out in the dirt, she stood up tall, and walked in as if she owned the damn place.

Her Majesty's Theatre!
June 3, 1843
SPECIAL ATTRACTION!

Mr. Benjamin Lumley begs to announce that, between the acts of the Opera, Donna Lola Montez will have the honor to make her first appearance in England in an Original Spanish dance!

Mr. Benjamin Lumley sat with Lola in his backstage office at Her Majesty's Theatre in London. "If you make a hit, you shall have a contract for the rest of the season. It all depends on yourself." Lola smiled and nodded to the man. She wanted nothing more. She left the managerial office and moved to the wings in a black satin bodice and flounced pink silk skirt. She waited for her cue, feeling as if she was treading on air. Lumley passed her one last time, giving her a nod of encouragement. "Capital," he said, rubbing his whiskers, "most attractive. You'll be a big success, my dear."

The conductor lifted his baton, and she took a deep breath. Everything had led up to this moment. The heavy curtains slowly were drawn aside and her heart began to race with excitement. Under watchful eyes through opera glasses, Lola floated onto the stage, opening the number with a beautiful pirouette. She executed her routine without flaw. There was a sudden hush at the finish of the number, she stepped up to the footlights and awaited the verdict. A storm of applause filled the air. Past the footlights, she could see Lumley from his place in the wings, he was beaming with approval.

Then, breaking her daydream, an ominous hiss suddenly split the air. It was coming from the occupants of the stage box of Lord Ranelagh. Lord Ranelagh shouted from the box "Egad!" in a loud voice. "That is not Lola Montez at all. It's the Irish Eliza Rosanna James, adulteress wife of Lieutenant James who had vanished! We're being properly swindled!" She rushed behind the curtain in tears, the audience was in an uproar. She was left penniless. Lola Montez fled to Prussia, when she then bore all to King Ludwig 1 and became a Bavarian Countess.

"To all men and women of every land, who are not afraid of themselves, who trust so much in their own souls that they dare to stand up in the might of their own individuality to meet the tidal currents of the world."

- Lola Montez - *The Arts of Beauty*

When Lola's identity had been revealed at Her Majesty's Theatre, it led to an arrest on a charge of bigamy. Lola's wealthy new husband George Trafford Heald bailed her out of jail and they ran to Spain. Her mother had found out about new life in Europe, and as if her daughter Eliza was dead, she went into mourning, sending out customary funeral letters on stationary edged in black. The feisty and sometimes violent Montez and Heald were not getting along and the couple eventually decided to split while in Portugal. George Heald then suddenly and "mysteriously" drowned and Lola gained Heald's large inheritance. Lola, with her new fortune, was ready to find a new start.

It was 1850, and she left for the land the whole world had been rushing to, The United States of America. On the stages up and down the east-coast of the New World, Lola Montez debuted her own gussied up version of a lively tarantella in tights the color of her flesh, and layers and layers of petticoats in every color that bounced with her quick, flirtatious steps. In this routine, she played the part of a maiden in the country with spiders in her clothes. The spiders hung from her gloves and gown and hid under the layers of her petticoat, which she shook off, layer by layer, exposing her shapely legs.

As she lifted her skirt, the men cheered for her to search for each and every spider. Lola lifted her petticoat so high that the men in the audience went crazy, for they could see that onstage, Lola wore no underclothing at all. Lola Montez was a smash. Although not everyone was impressed, and some believed her performance was unprofessional, and talentless. Lola stirred up excitement on that side of the new world for two years. After one particular show at a theatre on the East Coast, the manager openly criticized her spider act.

Backstage, the sassy star retaliated with the bullwhip that she used onstage. Lola busted the manager's face open with one lash. Denying the assault later, Lola had said, "There is one comfort in the falsehood, which is that this man very likely would have deserved the whipping."

Lola soon decided that she may be a better match with the lawless west, and without telling. Anyone, caught a ride via a Pacific Mail paddle-wheel steamer in New Orleans, headed for California. After the grueling passage along the isthmus of Panama, and finally on the last ship of the voyage, Lola stood on the deck with a male distinguished fellow passenger looking out over the water. He asked her about her life. "My father was Irish," she told him. "Irish! Well, then where did you get the name Montez?" Lola Montez stared out into the still ocean, "I took it." She said, "Just like I have taken everything I have ever wanted." He chuckled, approvingly.

The twenty-nine year old Lola was now an epic tabloid sensation in The United States. He knew exactly who she was. This man was Sam Brannan, California's first millionaire. Brannan was on his way home to his wife and four children after doing business in Boston and New York. He was paying a little too much attention to his glamorous shipmate for a married man. He kept her company, but truly, she was lonely. No one would be at the long wharf to greet her when she stepped off the ship into San Francisco in 1853. She was arriving unannounced.

On the north-east corner of Sansome and Halleck streets, stood the American Theater, the first brick large building built on the newly made soil along Sansome Street. The land had been reclaimed from Yerba Buena Cove. The Irish satirist Richard Brinsley Sheridan's comedy "School for Scandal" was playing, and Lola Montez was playing Lady Teazle. The theater was able to charge $5 for the best seats, an outrageous price. The reason being, the men in the audience truly desired to see her famous risqué Spider Dance they had read about in the East Coast papers. It was more than a dance they wanted to see.

Lola obliged on the second night, to the delight of the mostly male audience her body exposed by her contortions. She won the people over through naked charisma and pure force of personality. The act was well received by some, and had outraged others, who felt they were obliged to look for the spiders in improper places. Lola Montez was an eccentric woman who fascinated the masses entirely and straddled the fence between classes, rejecting the restrictive social rules of true womanhood.

Lola had the appearance of a Duchess but a personality and sense of humor considered even unacceptable even in the wee hours of the city's most provocative men's smoking clubs. She wore trousers and she carried a bullwhip. She had a fondness for hand-rolled cigarettes, and smoked openly, a habit that was unheard of for a lady. She was the first woman to ever be photographed while smoking. Although they watched her every move and even copied her style, San Francisco's respectable classes never truly embraced Lola Montez, and she really felt it.

Eventually, Lola and the married Sam Brannan reunited and she was being courted in a finer style then the Bavarian King Ludwig had ever provided her. That was quite an impressive feat. Sam Brannan had an income of one thousand dollars a day, which is over thirty-six thousand dollars in 2022. He owned over two hundred and fifty square miles in present day Los Angeles County. He lived well and lavishly, drinking and womanizing freely. His wife Ann eventually divorced Sam and when she did, she took half of everything he had. Lola moved on.

When Lola first sailed to San Francisco, on the same trip she met Brannan, she also met Patrick Purdy Hull, the Irish reporter and owner of the newspaper, The San Francisco Whig. Lola said Patrick Hull could tell a story better than any other man she had known, and that was why she fell in love with him. On July 1, 1853, at the Mission Dolores, Lola Montez and Patrick Hull were married in a catholic ceremony. Making Lola a US Citizen.

Lola left San Francisco for the unincorporated town of Grass Valley and bought a mine in a swelteringly hot ravine close next to Empire Mine and North Star Mine, two of the richest mines in Nevada Country, California. Lola Montez purchased the building at 248 Mill St in Grass Valley, the corner yard, covered in golden poppies. The house was constructed where Grass Valley held its first election under a large oak tree three years prior. It was first used as the office for Gilmore Meredith's Gold Hill Mining Company, and then as a schoolhouse. It made it the perfect home where her parrot, pet monkey, herself and Hull would live.

Grass Valley's Reverend spoke in a sermon denouncing Montez, he called her a hussy, and he called her evil. When Lola found out, she was furious. Deciding she would prove the quality of her act to the Reverend herself. That night, she stormed into the Reverend's house where he was sitting to eat dinner with his wife. Lola Montez demanded the couple watch her full performance. She stomped and clapped and shook around his living room until he finally agreed she was in fact, a professional.

The neighbors, who ran a boarding house, had a daughter who was fascinated with the clearly unique Lola Montez and her private menagerie and garden of golden poppies. It was not long before Lola was equally fascinated by the little girl, who was genuinely talented. Despite the townspeople's opinion, the mother of the girl liked Lola and appreciated the time she spent with her daughter. Patrick Hull was tired of the parties and extremely spiteful of his wife's popularity.

As with most of the relationships, Montez ended up hating her life with her newest husband and she rather spent her days with the young girl next door. The two rode horses and they watched the bald eagle who visited often. When a baron who was visiting from Europe attended one of Lola's social gatherings and gifted her a grizzly bear to add to her exotic collection of pets, Patrick Hull was insanely jealous, and this final straw ripped a tear in the relationship that could not be mended. She named the bear Major. Hull sued Montez for divorce, naming a German doctor as the co-respondent. A few days later, the doctor was found in near-by hills, shot dead.

In the two years that Lola lived in Grass Valley, the California Gold Rush was ending, but there was another gold mining rush in full swing in Australia. She hired Augustus Noel Folland, a married American actor as her new manager, hired a company of actors, and within two weeks, they were all sailing aboard the Fanny Major to Sydney. On the two month voyage, she took her new manager on as a lover.

The following week, Lola's show opened at the Royal Victoria Theatre in a show titled 'Lola Montez in Bavaria'. That night, Montez fired some of the company, and they quickly sued her for damages. As Lola and Folland, her manager and lover waited to depart Sydney, a sheriff's officer boarded the ship with a warrant of arrest, demanding she pay the sacked actors. Lola ran to her cabin, where she undressed. She sent out a note inviting the officer into her room to arrest her and drag her out in the nude. He left empty handed.

Montez brought out her Spider Dance when audiences began to diminish at the Theatre Royal in Melbourne. The papers roared that her performance was 'utterly subversive to all ideas of public morality'. The mayor of Melbourne was summoned to issue a warrant after a family complained about her public indecency.

Families stopped buying tickets and the show had heavy losses.

Months later in Ballarat, packed houses and miners were showering gold nuggets at her feet yet again, and yet again, the papers were attacking her notoriety. Lola by now had a motto. "Courage, and shuffle the cards." When Lola ran into a Ballarat Times editor, she retaliated by publicly horsewhipping him. The rest of her tour was canceled. Folland and Montez quarreled excessively as they left for San Francisco on May 22, 1856.

On the journey near Fiji on the night of July 8th, Folland "mysteriously" fell overboard and drowned. Some believed he committed suicide after their fight. Others believed he was pushed. No official investigation followed. When Lola arrived back in the United States in 1856, she was subdued. Whatever happened on that ship, changed Lola Montez. Alexandre Dumas, her previous lover from the past, once said, "Lola was fatal to any man who dares to love her."

Uncharacteristically, she sold her jewelry and gave the proceeds to Folland's children. She began using the remains of her bank account to give homeless and less fortunate women food, water and money. She decided to spread knowledge rather than performance, and began lecturing on her life, fashion, beauty, and famous women.

She began to write her book titled The Arts of Beauty, Or, Secrets of a Lady's Toilet: With Hints to Gentlemen on the Art of Fascinating.

"Dance with all the might of your body, and all the fire of your soul, in order that you may shake all melancholy out of your liver; and you need not restrain yourself with the apprehension that any lady will have the least fear that the violence of your movements will ever shake anything out of your brains. I never claimed to be famous. Notorious I have always been."

-Lola. Montez

She moved to New York, and reinvented herself once more, embracing christianity. Lola arranged to deliver a series of moral lectures written by Reverend Charles Chauncy Burr. She did her final lecture in Dublin speaking in Limerick and Cork, returning to America in 1859. Later that year, the Philadelphia Press wrote Lola "was living very quietly up town, and doesn't have much to do with the world's people. Some of her old friends, the Bohemians, now and then drop in to have a little chat with her, and though she talks beautifully of her present feelings and way of life, she generally, by way of parenthesis, takes out her little tobacco pouch and makes a cigarette or two for self and friend, and then falls back upon old times with decided gusto and effect. But she doesn't tell anybody what she's going to do."

Within two years, Lola Montez began showing the effects of syphilis, the last contribution to the marriage from Patrick Hurdy Hull, and her body began to waste away. Lola, 39 years old, suffered a massive stroke and died alone in poverty on January 7th, 1861. She is buried in the Greenwood cemetery, in Brooklyn.

The marker simply reads "Mrs. Eliza Gilbert - Died 7 January 1861." Lola's restored house at 248 Mill St. in Grass Valley is now a registered California Historical Landmark. Mount Lola, Nevada County and the Sierra Nevada's north of Interstate 80 highest point at 9,148 feet, is named in her honor as well as two lakes you can find in the Tahoe National Forest. Named the Upper and Lower Lola Montez Lakes. You may have heard this famous lyric - "Whatever Lola Wants, Lola Gets…" "Whatever Lola Wants" was written by Richard Adler and Jerry Ross for the 1955 musical play Damn Yankees. The saying was inspired by Lola Montez. Or what about "Her name was Lola, she was a showgirl, with yellow feathers in her hair and a dress cut down to there," even Copacabana by Barry Manilow was also inspired by our girl, Lola.

Richards, F. De B, photographer. *Lola Montez, three-quarter length studio portrait, facing left, wearing large lace shawl.* , None. [Place not identified: publisher not identified, between 1851 and 1853] Photograph. https://www.loc.gov/item/2015651568/.

Captivation

14

Firmly gripping the hand of her five year old daughter Charlotte, Mary Ann Crabtree, small in figure, scanned the sea of men that crowded the docks of San Francisco. She was looking for a familiar face. The face of her husband John, who had finally sent for them in New York. John Crabtree had left his family and position as a bookseller in New York and left for California in the search for gold in 1851. His wife and daughter dutifully waited for his call.

He finally wrote in 1853 and Mary Ann sold their bookshop off Broadway, and made the exhaustive journey to the Isthmus of Panama. They crossed by land before picking up a second ship to California, and now, John Crabtree was nowhere to be found.

In the Presidio of San Francisco, Charlotte and Mary Ann were given a temporary home with a group of popular actors, including Charlotte's new friend, the child actress Sue Robinson. The shrewd and thrifty woman zeroed in on the tantalizing theatre gossip and dreamt up a career of stardom for her cheerful, animated daughter Charlotte, or, like her mother called her, Lotta. Lotta had bright red hair, was sturdy with roguish black eyes and an unquenchable laughter. Yet Lotta was far off from stage ready.

During a celebration at her school near the Presidio, it was requested that Lotta sing 'Annie. Laurie' for the crowd. She barely made it to the platform before the young girl, to her mother's dismay, lost control and broke down, sobbing. She wept so hard and for so long, Mary Ann had to take her daughter home. That night in bed, Mary Ann went over her daughter's chances of success singing and dancing at the mines, ultimately doubting them.

The next morning, an optimistic letter came from her absent husband John vaguely mentioning prospecting in a town called Grass Valley. He requested that Mrs. Crabtree and Lotta proceed to him at once. Mary Ann, battling skepticism and the prospect of a bonanza, packed their belongings. At dawn, Lotta stood by the luggage as her mother procured a ride for two, and then they boarded the affordable, rickety stagecoach.

The young girl slept much of the journey. They were rolling into a torch lit shadowy settlement when she awoke. Lotta observed the intimidating shapes that danced across the walls of shacks, cast by the flickering torches and noticed the embers of a few dying fires, where the prospectors had woken up and started their day.

She was excited to see her father, it had been over two years since she had last seen him. She wondered if she would recognize him as he went to hug her? Her hopes were crushed when they met him on Main Street in Grass Valley. There was no embrace, John embraced his wife and patted Lotta's head before turning to walk ahead as he took them to a hotel where the family shared a small bed for the night.

That next morning, the family took a walk among the poppies to admire what the high Sierra spring had to offer. Men were attending their claims in an air of conquest, working tirelessly digging tunnels, sinking shafts, bridging gorges, and piping water in flumes across the foothills. John told his family stories of men literally stumbling upon rich mines, pulling gold out of the earth with a knife, and how he once left a claim prior to the "big strike." Nestled in the rich green slopes and fertile deep gullies, Lotta saw the promise of luck, as the melting snow fed streams with the clearest water she had ever seen.

They passed by peddlers offering sealing wax, baubles, trinkets, and luxurious fabrics. Lotta approached a man that sold paperbacks, and ran her finger down the spine of a Dickens novel. She noticed if a vendor was not prosperous enough to possess mules, they carried their goods strapped into a pack that was worn on the shoulders.

As Lotta looked at the books, John asked his wife "Why not keep a boarding house? Everyone spends lavishly here, and rich merchants in town need homes! We could do no less than get rich." Mary Ann was disappointed, she was not familiar in the kitchen. In New York, she worked in upholstery and had a servant who did the household work and cooked. She agreed.

To Mary Ann's surprise, she did a fantastic job maintaining the boarding house. Not to her surprise, John's participation quickly diminished and he wandered away to prospect. But luck had not been with John Crabtree. With all the excitement around them, John Crabtree only offered Mary Ann disappointment. Mary Ann continued her duties and began to save her money. That summer, a global sensation moved into a lot near the

Crabtrees. The new neighbor soon transformed the home into a true salon that was constantly booming with singing and laughter. Lotta soon attracted the attention of the eccentric woman who had a pet parrot and a monkey.

Mary Ann had always kept her daughter Lotta under her watchful eye and by doing so, Lotta's life had been incredibly innocent. Now, Mary Ann was entirely lenient while Lotta was in company with this new, famous companion and Lotta Crabtree and Lola Montez bonded instantly. In the parlor of the Montez home, Lola was constantly impressed, Lotta had a better sense of rhythm than Lola. There were daily singing lessons and Lola taught Lotta fandangos, intricate ballet steps, and the jigs reels and Irish flings from her own childhood.

Lotta was allowed to play in Lola's trunk of stage costumes, and operate Lola's German music box. They did not stop indoors, Lola also taught Lotta to ride horseback. The child's bubbly personality fit right in as she mingled with the trolling players, entertainers and witty theatrical company who came to visit her new best friend, the star.

On one sunny morning, the two went for a ride. Lola rode a horse and Lotta was on a pony. They ended up in the town of Rough and Ready, where huge fortunes were recklessly gambled away. The street was lined with gaming houses and saloons boasting bullet-riddled ceilings. Lola and Lotta sauntered into the busiest saloon. Lola stood Lotta on a blacksmith's anvil, and the young child danced for the group of cheering miners. Irishmen made up a sizable fraction of the miners in Rough and Ready and Lotta's jigs had reminded them of home. They threw more than a generous amount of gold nuggets at her feet. The child was a refreshing change in entertainment for the men. Lola brought the gold home to Mary Ann and declared Lotta should go with her to Paris.

The next morning, John reappeared without warning with the news that they were moving to Rabbit Creek, forty miles north of Grass Valley. Mary Ann was not happy. Compared to the somewhat civilized, law-abiding Grass Valley, Rabbit Creek was a small but busy and violent camp. Murders were frequent, as each pocket of gold was found. Mary Ann was reluctant, but went along with his plan, and turned down Montez's proposition. When the family arrived in Rabbit Creek, there was an intense drought that summer which affected the prospectors, who needed water for washing gold. John chose to spend his time drinking in the saloons and rambling away mysteriously on quote unquote prospecting missions, no gold was found.

Months went by without her husband's support and Mary Ann's only option was to open another boarding house. She opened up that winter, around the same time that Mart Taylor, an Italian musician and dancer, arrived in Rabbit Creek. Taylor was tall and had a graceful figure, with long hair and piercing black eyes. He opened a saloon with a connecting makeshift theatre where Taylor conducted a dancing school for children when the business slowed down in the afternoon.

His first prerequisite was music and he was impressed by the 8 year old red-haired Lotta, who looked younger than she was by two years. Her eyes would flash as her small feet traced the intricate steps Lola taught her. A child performer would be a fun, fresh show for the audiences of miners. Lotta would be a sensation.

Taylor hired a fiddler and played the guitar on his makeshift theatre stage. Mrs. Crabtree played the triangle and Lotta entertained the miners. Lotta would often get stage fright, and it would show when she shoved her hands in her pockets.

Few child stars had training, and Lotta, was trained by Lola Montez. Lotta Crabtree had become a Rabbit Creek nightly attraction, wearing a custom made outfit by Mary Ann, consisting of green tail-coat, knee breeches, tall hat and brogans with pockets that her mother had sewn shut. She danced jig after jig, only pausing to change costumes, she would return to a storm of applause to then sing a ballad for a finale. Lotta Crabtree would shake the house with emotion, and the gold nuggets shone at her feet. Naturally, Mrs. Crabtree became her daughter's manager and the Crabtree family now had more money than ever. Lotta was a gold mine.

Lola Montez rode over to Rabbit Creek to see her protege and talk to her mother/manager. Lola was going on tour to Australia and she wanted to bring little Lotta with her. Mary Ann declined, she saw a future for Lotta with Mart Taylor and Mary Ann used Lola's request to take the child to Australia to her advantage which helped Lotta's growing reputation. That summer, Mary Ann discovered that she was to have another child and Lotta's baby brother, John Ashworth, was born, just as John Sr. returned home.

Lotta continued to work for Taylor while her mother recovered from the birth. After years of performing in Rabbit Creek, the next move seemed obvious to Mary Ann. Lotta should tour the mines.

On a late spring morning in 1856, Mary Ann left her husband John three loaves of fresh bread, a kettle of beans and a goodbye note. Lotta sat next to her mother with her baby brother in her arms in the wagon as they left with Taylor's troupe. As they toured in the California mining camps, on a makeshift stage set up on sawhorses with candles stuffed into bottles serving as footlights arranged along the outer edge for an audience of men whom Lotta had never seen before, she began to make a name for herself.

Mary Ann Crabtree used the knowledge that she had picked up from the actors she met in the Presidio and at the home of Montez. She distrusted theatre folk at heart but would listen to every word, resisting its attraction. Mary Ann mistrusted theatre folk, but she did not mistrust the theatre itself. Mary Ann always had to give Lotta a little push to get her on the stage, needing to coax Lotta by telling her funny stories and persuading her for an hour or more before it was time for the stage. Once onstage, Lotta would perfectly execute her routine.

At every performance's conclusion, Lotta would appear angelically, a face scrubbed clean, hair smoothly combed, a white dress with puffed sleeves. Mary Ann, exhausted from costuming, coaching, and playing the triangle, then collected the gold in a basket, scraping every fragment of dust from the boards. Mary Ann and Lotta never had a moment to relax, even while riding to the next town. They overcame many obstacles on the road beyond the trees that snapped and blocked their path as they traveled the dangerous High Sierra by horseback. At one point they nearly missed a boulder that was rolling down the mountain side after being loosened by mining operations. Eight year old Lotta watched as a lone rider plunged into the bottom of an abyss in front of her eyes. After one performance, Lotta lay ducked on the floor with her mother, in their room, as bullets burst through the canvas walls while a brawl in the hotel commenced. Yet Mary Ann remained cool, and kept Lotta in good spirits.

As busy as Mary Ann was, she still found time to become pregnant again, with another younger brother for Lotta. Taylor's company was then forced to break up in Weaverville. Mark Taylor took Lotta's brother, Ashworth Jr. to San Francisco and Lotta was sent to stay with the pioneer family of James Ryan Talbot in Eureka, where Lotta thoroughly enjoyed a normal childhood while her mother had the new baby.

In 1856 Mary Ann traveled to Eureka to gather Lotta and her belongings. Mary Ann, Lotta and her newest brother, George then caught a schooner to San Francisco. San Francisco had grown to bold proportions, with longer wharves, and elaborate buildings and it did not seem to be the same city Mary Ann left years ago. Gamblers crowded the halls, natives rode on spirited horses through the streets, and silk lined carriages dashed around. It had become legendarily violent. Charles Cora had just been hanged for the murder of the United States Marshal Richardson by the second Vigilance Committee, yet the days of lawlessness were not yet gone. The exuberant scene was exciting for Mary Ann, and Lotta was more than impressed.

Lotta followed her mother into the Bella Union, mesmerized by the women in lurid clothes, dealing cards to a group of shady men. Taken backstage quickly, Lotta performed, Mary Ann got paid, and took her away, hoping the wild atmosphere of the saloon did not leave an impression. Mary Ann was booking Lotta all over the city, enforcing the hard bargains she drove, hungry for gold yet still protecting Lotta passionately. When they left the Bella Union, Lotta saw an eagle overhead, and thought of her friend Lola and her bear Major and longed for a normal childhood. Mary Ann started booking Lotta for acting gigs.

When Lotta appeared in The Dumb Belle, Lotta was to carry a bottle onstage, place it on a table and exit. There was an older actress who insisted on having the role but Mrs. Crabtree was sure to not let it happen. Mary Ann showed Lotta how to do an elaborate pantomime. The audience showered the stage with money and roared with laughter. Lotta wasn't going anywhere. She had a great power to draw an audience.

The family started touring, traveling by schooner across the bay, then up shallow Petaluma Creek, carrying Lotta's costumes in champagne baskets, and Lotta's earnings in gold, in a large leather bag. Lotta made good profits in Sonoma County and she was now in demand in the Sacramento and San Joaquin Valleys. The shrewd Mary Ann did not trust banks nor paper money. When the bag became too heavy it was transferred to a steamer trunk. When the steamer trunk became too heavy, Mary Ann invested Lotta's earnings in local real estate, race horses and bonds.

Like her dear friend Lola, Lotta began smoking small, thinly rolled black cigars. She often, on stage and off, wore male clothes. Appearing unladylike became a trademark for Lotta. She gained a new skill when a skilled black breakdown dancer taught her a vigorous and complicated soft-shoe dance in Placerville. Lotta could also laugh at herself. She once slipped in the street and called out "prima donna in the gutter". All of this kept her out of the prominent ladies social group, Sorosis. Lotta wanted nothing to do with the ladies in the group and this infuriated Mary Ann.

By 1859, she mastered the suggestive double entendre long before Mae Wes and had become "Miss Lotta, the San Francisco Favorite." She played in Virginia City, and the famous Bird Cage Theater in Tombstone, Arizona. Followed by a tour on the east-coast, performing in plays at theaters. She was a favorite for her portrayals of children due to her petite size.

The New York Times called her "The eternal child" with "The face of a beautiful doll and the ways of a playful kitten," and that No" one could wriggle more suggestively than Lotta". They also said, in reference to her skills as a dancer, "What punctuation is to literature, legs are to Lotta". By the end of the decade the "Lotta Polka" and "Lotta Gallup" were quite the rage in the United States. Lotta sat down to write a letter to a friend in San Francisco in 1865.

"We started out quite fresh, and so far things have been very prosperous. I am a continual success wherever I go. In some places I created quite a theatrical furor, as they call it. I have played with the biggest houses but never for so much money, for their prices are double. I'm a star, and that is sufficient, and I am making quite a name. But I treat each and every one with the greatest respect and that is not what everyone does, and in consequence I get my reward."

Four years later, Lotta purchased a lot on the south-side of Turk Street, east of Hyde, paying seven thousand dollars, just a portion of her earnings at a recent show. In September of 1875 she gave the city of San Francisco a gift of appreciation to the people. It was a fountain modeled after a lighthouse prop from one of her plays at the intersection of Market and Kearny streets. Politicians, respectable citizens and even hellions gathered to dedicate the city's new public drinking fountain.

She began touring the nation with her own theatrical company that year, hitting the height of her success for a full decade. Lotta was still only a teenager, shocking audiences by showing her legs and smoking on stage. Mary Ann was still managing her career, finding locations, organizing troupes of actors and booking plays for the then highest-paid actress in America, who was earning sums of up to five thousand. Dollars per week.Lotta had many admirers and was proposed to many times but never married.

From newspaper boys, European royalty, to lawyers and well known actors, Lotta time after time turned them down. She said, "I'm married to the stage." Some said her mother would not allow it as it would end her ability to be considered forever young, and her career left little time for a social life. Some say she was only interested in women. It was whispered in the backstages of the theaters that Adah Isaacs Menken was Lotta's secret lover. Lotta was a bit of a rebel in her day, advocating women's rights and wearing skirts too short while laughing at society matrons.

In New Orleans, Lotta was presented with a gold medal and a beautiful banjo by "The Lotta Baseball Club." Lotta was also close with many other celebrities, including President Abraham Lincoln and his wife and the great Harry Houdini. President Ulysses S. Grant always made it a point to visit her whenever she was performing in Washington DC while he was president. Her friend, the actor John Barrymore, referred to Lotta as "The Queen of the American stage."

Lotta traveled to Europe with her mother and brothers, learning French, visiting museums and taking up painting. After her tour ended, she went home to San Francisco to perform at the California Theatre. The people of San Francisco missed their very own star while she was away. In 1883, The New York Times devoted much of its front page to "The Loves of Lotta."

In 1885, Mary Ann had an eighteen room summer cottage built on the shores of Lake Hopatcong in Breslin Park at Mount Arlington, New Jersey. It was a gift for her daughter Lotta. The Queen Anne/Swiss chalet style lakefront estate sat on land that sloped down to Van Every Cove, so there are 2-1/2 stories on the land side and 3-½ stories on the lake side. The home's "upside-down" chimneys had corbels that flared outward near the top. She named it Attol Tryst (Lotta spelled backward). There was an expansive porch, including a semi-circular section that traced the curve of the parlor, wrapping around three sides of the house. Inside, there was a wine cellar, music room, library, and a fireplace flanked by terra cotta dog-faced beasts. The billiard room's massive stone fireplace once featured a mosaic that spelled out LOTTA in gemstones. They threw parties there, rode horses, and pursued her painting.

Lotta had a terrible fall in the spring of 1889 while in Wilmington, Delaware. Lotta recovered lakeside and decided to retire permanently from the stage, at age 45. She resisted calls for a farewell tour. She was the richest actress in America and had made quite a spectacle as one of the first women to own and drive her own car that she called "Red Rose."

She got out on top. During her retirement, Lotta traveled, painted and was active in charitable work. One final appearance was made in 1915 for Lotta Crabtree Day in San Francisco at the Panama-Pacific Exposition. Lotta was a vegetarian for years and took time to visit inmates in prisons. Boston papers recalled Lotta as a devoted animal rights activist who wandered the streets, putting hats on horses to protect them from the sun.

When Mary Ann died, Lotta's serious side emerged. Lotta seriously wanted to have Mary Ann sainted. But she eventually settled on having a twenty-thousand dollar stained glass window decorated with angels made for her, which is today in St. Stephen's church in Chicago. The last 15 years of Lotta's life was spent living alone at the Brewster Hotel, which she had purchased in Boston, a dog at her feet, regularly traveling to Gloucester to paint seascapes, with a cigar in her teeth.

Lotta Crabtree died at home on September 25, 1924 at age 76 and she was interred at the Woodlawn Cemetery in Bronx, New York. She was described by critics as a tease, mischievous, unpredictable, impulsive, rattlebrained, cheerful and devilish. Lotta's Fountain still stands at the intersection of Market and Kearny streets in San Francisco, the oldest surviving monument in the City's collection. After the earthquake, Lotta's Fountain was a known gathering place and one of the only locations to get potable water in the city. It is the site of the anniversary of the 1906 San Francisco earthquake every April 18th.

Lotta left an estate of some $4 million in a charitable trust for Anti-Animal Experimentation, a trust to provide food, fuel and hospitalization for the poor and to assist in the aide of released convicts, and to support the poor, needy actors. Also, to help young graduates of agricultural colleges and relief for needy vets of WWI. The trust still exists today.

The estate ran into complications when a number of people claiming to be relatives unsuccessfully contested the will. Friend of the Crabtree family, famed Wyatt Earp even testified at one of the hearings. One woman claimed to be Lotta's adult child. A long series of court hearings followed. A medical exam was conducted at the autopsy and it was confirmed that Lotta Crabtree had never had sex with a man. There is no known video or audio of her performing. She was the queen of the stage, but retired before the days of Hollywood. Lotta's influence is all around us today in the domino of effects from the money and support she has given to farmers, animals, prisoners, soldiers, and actors. Her strong influence on animal rights, women's rights, and human rights have forever shaped society and she left a legacy of love with fountains, paintings, and by promoting the arts. Lotta started the tradition of daytime performances for women and children, now commonly known as the afternoon matinee. Lotta was not about wars, but very supportive of the members of the military, and America. Lotta has been credited as being an influence to Mary Pickford, Mae West, Betty Hutton, and Judy Garland. The Academy Award nominated 1951 movie musical "Golden Girl" was based on Lotta's exciting life, starring Hollywood Walk-Of-Famer, Mitzi Gaynor as Lotta. Crabtree Hall, a dormitory at the University of Massachusetts Amherst, is named for Lotta. The Attol Tryst stands today and in recent years it has been restored.

Gurney & Son, photographer. *Lotta Crabtree, full-length portrait, facing right, smoking cigar*. ca. 1868. Photograph. https://www.loc.-gov/item/2005690001/

The Brave Stage Driver
15

Imagine driving six horses pulling a full stagecoach carrying passengers, supplies, mail, and gold down an improvised treacherous dirt trail in the blistering sun or through freezing rain and snow. Envision controlling the whole operation as you twisted over mountain passes, along narrow cliffs and over swollen streams. You would have to be good with a gun to keep your cargo safe and your passengers alive. You would speed through dense forests into canyons of wild bear, mountain lions, thieving bandits and rattlesnakes, because you had to arrive on time.

For the first 20 years of California's history, stagecoaches, wagons, pack-mules, horses and walking were the only modes of transportation. Driving Stage in the menacing country was a risky job in a treacherous era. Stage drivers were the Gold Rush road-warriors. It was said that Wyatt Earp, Wild Bill Hickok, and Buffalo Bill Cody, all had driven stage coaches. In the late spring of 1851, San Francisco was burning. Tens of millions of dollars in damage had been done. Charley Parkhurst was in Panama, crossing the isthmus shortcut, on his way to California via the city that was burning, unbeknownst to him. The passengers on board the R.B. Forbes from Boston was perplexed by Charley.

"He calls himself Charles Clifton but passengers on board call him Thunderbolt. In the crowded passenger quarters, He says the reason for passing under an assumed name was that he was an important witness in a case and wished to have nothing to do with it, adopting a false name to get out of the way. In short, he was a very queer fellow indeed!"

-The European traveler John Charles Duchow

During the voyage, Charley met John Morton of Morton Warehouse Company of San Francisco. The two made fast friends. Parkhurst told Morton about his previous boss Birch, who had given him the idea to come to California. Charley told Morton what he told Birch, "I aim to be the best damn driver in California." John Morton quickly realized Charley was the toughest and most tenacious man on the trail, and recruited him to be the Morton Warehouse Company's stagecoach driver once they arrived in California.

When the time came to disembark in San Francisco, it was a cool summer evening. Thirty-nine year old Charley adjusted his pleated shirt and his long gloves as he walked down the gangplank of the pier and saw a burnt down, demolished San Francisco that was hastily being rebuilt. It was a sight to see.
After working for a short time in the developing city for the Morton Warehouse Company of San Francisco, Charley decided to go north to Sacramento. He was anxiously looking for his former boss from Georgia, James E. Birch. Birch had started his stagecoach service at 21, in the busy town as a driver with one wagon and was now building several small stage lines known as the California Stage Company.

He arrived in Sacramento and sauntered down the dusty Main Street. He had not seen his old friend since Birch left for California. He stepped up onto the wooden path and swung the door of the California Stage Company open. Inside, Birch was in the middle of questioning several potential drivers. Charley stood and observed as Birch questioned the men.

"How close could you allow the stage to get to a thousand-foot drop and be sure the passengers would be safe?" One man yelled, "Two feet!" another said, unsure, "Five inches?" and a third boasted, "I could make it with half the tire hanging over the edge." Charley was appalled, and yelled "I'd stay as far away from the edge of that cliff as the hubs would let me" and headed for the door, to come back another time. Charley did not make it out of the building before Birch grabbed his stout shoulders from behind him, turned him around and shook the hand of his 5 foot friend, grinning. "Charley! The job is yours." Charley smiled back, his lips stained from chewing tobacco.

At work, Charley frequently slept with the horses and rose before dawn each morning to put his team in a particular order, the order playing to each of the horses' strengths. He joked, "I get along better with horses than folks." When the sun rose, the street would be lined with more than fifty wagons and coaches loaded with passengers, the latest news, mail to be delivered, and gold to be banked, all ready to head to the camps and mining towns in the Sierra Nevadas and it's foothills.

When Charley's stagecoach arrived into the little towns, it caused much excitement. Children would run about chaotically, mobbing the driver for the candy he had stashed in the wagon for moments like this. It took a certain type of man to ignore the temptations of the 1850s and hold this grueling job. Charley was always dependable. On occasion, Charley would pull double duty through the night in dangerous conditions in the rain and snow. When the roads were nearly impassable, he would drive regardless and use mud-wagons, to get to the wild boomtowns of Rough and Ready, Grass Valley, Stockton, Mariposa, Placerville, Santa Cruz and "the great stage route" from San Jose to Oakland, earning double pay.

On a hot afternoon in Redwood City, Charley's lead horse Pete was growing skittish. Charley pulled the team over and climbed out to soothe ol'Pete. Charley was approaching the horse from the carriage when he heard a rattler in the bush shake its tail. Startled, Pete kicked Charley, square in the temple, the accident cost Charley an eye. Despite being half blind, Charley developed a reputation as one of the finest stagecoach drivers on the West Coast, and was celebrated as "the most dexterous and best of the California drivers." He spoke with a rasp, drank whiskey with the best of them and could handle himself in a fistfight. He earned the nickname 'One-Eyed Charley' and wore a black eye patch over his clean shaven face, a strange choice in those days.

The first alleged non-indigenous discoverer of the Yosemite Valley was James Savage. In 1848, Savage had claimed an area near there, then simply called Savage's Diggings, where he had discovered gold. Now known as Big Oak Flat, The method of punishment for crime nearby was often hanging at a huge oak tree in the camp named Garrote. Garrote was a Spanish word for execution by strangulation, and Garrote is now known as Groveland.

Wiping the rushing water from his face, Charley guided the coach through the mud. The rain had been coming down in sheets for the last three days as Charley Parkhurst made his way to Savage's Diggings in his coach from Stockton. Up ahead, there was a stray man on the trail, waving his arms wildly. Charley stopped the stage. The man jogged to the coach and yelled over the storm. "Do not cross the bridge right now sir, the thaw was extra heavy on the Tuolumne River this spring and the bridge is shaky and unstable! I insist!" Charley tipped his hat at the stranger and cracked the reins and kept on until they approached the roaring, swollen stream. Moments later, the bridge just below Big Oak Flat revealed itself, it was nearly washed out. Time was of the essence.

The stagecoach had one passenger with him, and the man pleaded with his driver to stop. Charley clenched his teeth and tightened his grip on the reins, like a natural, he viciously swung his long whip upon his team, and the stage dashed across the creaking structure, the planks trembling under horses' hooves and the coaches wheels. They took on the swollen Tuolumne River and the turbulent waters ripped the bridge away, just as the wheels reached the solid ground. "I thought we were goners for sure." Charley's passenger said as he removed his hat and wiped his brow, The brave stage driver did not even look up from the road ahead of him when he said, "Well friend, I would never let that happen, as I am particular about who I take a bath with."

And that was the truth.

In the 1820s, Ebenezer Balch owned a livery stable in Providence, Rhode Island when he met twelve year old Charley Parkhurst, an orphan who was admiring Balch's horses on the streets of Worcester, MA. Charley had carefully watched every move made by the stage drivers of Worcester and was eager to learn all he could about horses. Balch, an encouraging fellow, and took him home, promising to make a man out of Charley. After earning his keep cleaning stalls, washing carriages and scrubbing floors, the runaway began to learn the art of driving horse-drawn carriages, first one-in-hand, then two-in-hand, then four-in-hand, and eventually, six-in-hand. Charley prospered there and a reputation was made, known as one of the best coachmen on the eastern seaboard.

In 1812, just over a decade before that, a poor, young couple in Vermont, Mary and Ebenezer Parkhurst had three children, Maria, Charlotte, and Charles. When one of the Parkhurst's three children suddenly passed away, the couple abandoned the other two, who ended up in an orphanage in Lebanon, New Hampshire. The children were raised under the care of an unkind man named Mr. Millshark. Charlotte, the youngest of the two, became aware that women had few economic opportunities and that men had a greater advantage over girls in the battle of life. She felt her only future as a girl was to be a seamstress, laundress, teacher or sex worker. So, when she was 12 years old, Charlotte left Maria, her older sister at the orphanage, stole a few pieces of boys clothing and ran away to Worcester, MA. Charlotte then took on the name of her deceased brother, Charles, or, Charley Parkhurst.

Before traveling to California on a cold winter night while still working back east, Charley sat on his stage outside of a dance waiting for his passengers to return. As the night went on, the icy night air caused Charley's delicate hands to freeze. He was humiliated. How would he explain he would be unable to drive? Charley's proud friend Liberty Childs, a fellow driver, took over the route. The teasing began. It was not long after Charley was rescued from the cold that he left for California, with long-fingered, beaded buckskin gloves to hide and protect his fragile hands.

Charley did have a fantastic record until in California, Charley was driving his six horses across rough terrain with a money box full of gold and a coach full of passengers. He has been going for hours, unaware that bandits lay in wait. Charley was focused on a sharp and steep bend in the trail, when a group of men who wore masks made out of long underwear, surrounded the stage, stopping them on the cliff.

The bandits were the notorious "Sugarfoot" and his crew. As the crew crowded in on the passengers, yelling threats, Sugarfoot put his gun to Charley's temple, his good one. The cry of an eagle rang out. His grey eye looked alert, straight ahead. Parkhurst always carried a brace of pistols stuck in his belt, and was not afraid to use them. He could slice open the end of an envelope or cut a cigar out of a man's mouth from twenty feet away, but his gun was out of reach. In order to protect his passengers from the rough gang, Charley kicked over the wagon's strong box, which contained the valuables of all the passengers onboard. As the bandits rode down the trail behind them, Parkhurst yelled out to Sugarfoot and his men. If I ever see you again, it will be unpleasant.

And then there was that one afternoon on the Carson Pass. As Charley drove down the steep terrain, the lead horses suddenly veered from the trail, jerking the wagon so severely it tossed Charley out of the wagon and into a bed of golden poppies. The horses went full speed, as he clung to the reins, dragging Parkhurst along, face down. For a moment the team slowed down enough for Charley to get on his feet, running next to the coach and finally leaping up to his seat. The passengers took a sigh of relief as Charley, unaffected, steered the frightened horses back onto the road.

His solid work inspired Wells Fargo to trust Charley with special missions. On one of these missions, Charley drove late into the night, on a steep and rough mountain pass. "I've traveled over these mountains so often I can tell where the road is by the sound of the wheels. When they rattle, I'm on hard ground; when they don't rattle, I generally look over the side to see where she's a-going."

As the stage rattled along, Charley saw Sugarfoot, the same notorious road agent, waiting in the path to stop Charley again. Charley chuckled to himself and in defiance, he cracked his whip. It would be the last robbery this thief ever attempted. The team of horses charged, and Sugarfoot dove out of the way. Charley pulled out his revolver and as he passed the criminal, he turned, and fired. Sugarfoot, hit, crawled to a nearby cabin owned by a miner. Inside, they saw he had a bullet wound in his stomach. Sugarfoot, drifting into his death, mumbled, "I'been shot by the famous driver, One-eyed Charley."

Wells Fargo, impressed by Parkhurst's bravery, presented Parkhurst with a large watch and chain made of solid gold in appreciation. When the railroad was rapidly replacing the stagecoach, Parkhurst made the decision to give up driving, and opened and operated a ranch, horse changing station and saloon halfway between Santa Cruz and Watsonville. He later raised cattle on Bean Creek with Frank Woodward. In the winters, Charley would supplement his income by logging in Hungry Hollow in the mountains of Santa Cruz, working for and living with Andy Jackson Clark and his family.

He would earn five dollars a day when younger men earned only three. For fifteen years Charley worked these laboring jobs, finally selling his business, saving several thousands of dollars to retire on. Just before he left though, stone cold drunk one evening, Andy's wife asked her seventeen-year-old son to put Charley to bed. The teenager obeyed and after he assisted the man into his room, and helped him change out of his boots and such, the boy returned in shock, "Maw, Charley, ain't no man, he's a woman!" Mrs. Clark and her son respected Charley's choice, and never mentioned it to a soul.

Charley moved onto the Moss Ranch, sixty miles north of Watsonville in a small cabin owned by the Harman Family. In the early part of 1879, he began to complain of a sore throat that never went away. The Harman's begged Charley to visit the doctor, but Charley was stubborn, and old fashioned. For Charley's whole life, to avoid the doctor, he would treat himself in one of two ways, either use the same remedies he would on his horses, or take the leftover medicine from a friend.

"I'm no better now than when I commenced. Pay's small and work's heavy. I'm getting old. Rheumatism in my bones — nobody to look out for old used-up stage drivers. I'll kick the bucket one of these days and that'll be the last of old Charley."

Rheumatism eventually shriveled Charley's limbs, and due to the pain in his throat, he finally consented to be taken to a doctor, who diagnosed his condition as cancer of the tongue and throat. Dr. Plumm recommended an operation to insert a silver tube or pipe in the throat but Charley wanted nothing to do with anything of the sort. On several instances during his stay with the Harman family, he said he had something to tell them but he kept postponing the telling until eventually it was too late, as he could no longer talk.

Frank Woodward, his friend and business partner had kept vigil at Charley's side while he succumbed to his cancer, he died on December 18, 1879, leaving strict instructions to be buried in the clothes he was wearing. His friends and neighbors however, insisted on washing the body, and came to the cabin to prepare the body for burial. It was then discovered that Charley Parkhurst was born a woman.

As the examining doctor finished up, he then told the Harman's, that Charley in fact at once gave birth at some time, and their son found his will, where Charley left $600.00 to a "George". Charley's locked tin trunk, which contained a red dress and a pair of baby shoes.

The discovery of Charley's true sex became a national sensation. At what point did Charley have a daughter? Was he really an important witness in the court case, like he had told others? Or was it a lack of opportunity for adventurous work as a woman? For we can assume that Parkhurst would not have become a famous stagecoach driver as a woman. It is possible that if Charley was alive today, he would identify as transgender. One could use he/him or they/them as a pronoun for Parkhurst. Charley was an active agent in asserting a gendered self, for most of his life. He was he, and queerness and transness is something that's been around in some form everywhere, for always.

The 19th Amendment was passed by Congress June 4, 1919, and ratified on August 18, 1920, granting women the right to vote. More than 52 years before this, Charley Parkhurst registered to vote in Santa Cruz. The Santa Cruz Sentinel of October 17, 1868 lists Parkhurst's name as recorded on the official poll list for the election of 1868. The voting records from that year were burned in a fire, so we will never know, but if Charley did vote that year, he may very well have been the first being, born a woman, to vote in a presidential election in California. You can visit the Famous, fearless, adventurous stage driver's grave today at the Pioneer Cemetery at 44 Main Street in Watsonville, California. There is a plaque at his grave, as well as at the Soquel Fire Station and Soquel Post Office, commemorating Charley as the first woman to vote in the United States of America.

Exhilaration
16

Simone Jules, the daughter of a French Viscount, was virtually imprisoned in a chateau in the south of France in a miserable marriage to an overbearing man. After Napoleon's fall, her father returned to find his estate and finances in ruins. It had been set up by her father in a last effort to restore a family fortune. Simone longed to escape her situation in France for over a year and found herself in a romantic entanglement with a Lieutenant. The affair swiftly ended her marriage and when Simone Jules had the chance to leave, she took it, and left France for good.

In San Francisco, on the west of Kearney Street, stood the infamous Bella Union Hotel and it featured shows of all varieties, gambling, drinking and dancing. An eager man wandered into the smoke and debauchery in the back of The Bella Union's gambling hall. He saw a petite French woman with smokey eyes and raven hair pulled back from her round face of olive skin dealing a card game like a professional. A female dealer was then unheard of. He approached the table, the game was Vingt-et-un, almost completely unknown in California at the time.

Originating in the French Casinos in the early 1700s, in English they call it "21". With a sweet smile, she asked him, "*You will play, monsieur?*" The man blushed, and twisted with embarrassment, for he had no money to gamble. The gorgeous woman winked at him, her eyes sparkling in their jetty blackness. The dealer then gracefully gestured for a staff member to bring out a meal to the man. She then turned back to her players, who handed over their money, in a trance, obviously enamored by the nineteen year old French gal's wit and charm.

A heavy plate of oysters, hard boiled eggs and potatoes arrived at the man's table. He ate his meal, appalled by her generosity, studied the delicate woman and the connection she had with her patrons. She was dignified, elegant, and handled the rowdy locals with ease. During his meal, a loud boisterous gambler got out of hand, she made it obvious that she was not one to be bullied and had the man quickly removed. As another gambler lost every last cent at her table, the dining man shoved a forkful of potatoes in his mouth and watched in awe as the dealer bought the losing man a glass of milk.

Simone Jules dealing cards at the Bella Union proved to bring in an incredible amount of business, and she was earning quite a bit of money as well. The other halls quickly noticed and began to hire women. The other dealers at the Bella Union began to grow jealous of Jules' success. They found an alliance and decided to accuse Simone of being a clever card shark. Jules was accused of being a cheater who skinned her victims as she smiled at them, and consequently, she was fired from the Bella Union.

Simone decided to work closer to the mines, the men who worked them, and the gold they were finding. With her own bag of gold, she headed 140 miles east to the Sierra Nevada Mountains, to the once sleepy Spanish town of Nevada City. The name Nevada, in Spanish, translates to snow-covered. On the daily stagecoach that ran between Nevada City and Sacramento, she told a fellow traveler of her plans to open a lavish gambling palace. "Oh honey," the bearded man told her, "you gotta be real careful, the bonanzas brought desperate men and they are mad to get rich and they won't hesitate to poison your drink or slit your throat for your purse." She stared out the window of the stagecoach, asking herself, "Did I survive the devil sierras to get murdered in Nevada City?"

Nevada City had been in a boom for the past five years and men had fled in from all over the world to get rich off the high grade ore that flowed in the rivers. The gold, then transferred to a leather pouch, soon to be measured and traded for whiskey or female companionship. She looked out the carriage window, watching the men roam around in an alcoholic haze. Simone Jules noticed immediately that the town lacked sophistication when her stagecoach rolled into town, down the crowded street in 1854.

As the stage rolled to a stop, it became obvious to Jules that women were few. She stepped out of the coach, and her appearance created much commotion among the rough men. Who was she? That evening, when she checked into the Fepps Hotel, she registered under the name Eleanor Dumont. As she unpacked her personals, she giggled to herself, pleased. In San Francisco, her appearance as a stylish woman had never attracted as much attention. The mystery of the French woman was solved in her second week in Nevada City, when the town arose to a handbill covered town. The handbills announced the grand opening of Madame Eleanore Dumont's Gaming Parlor.

On the door of the newest and most elegant gambling hall in Nevada City, stenciled in gold lettering, read "Dumont's - A Gambling Establishment For Gentlemen Only". Resting men, lounged on the finest furniture, partaking in rare and choice wines and liqueurs. At Dumont's, a dozen gambling games led by an honest dealer kept going night and day. Win or lose, there was more satisfaction in playing against the polite and smiling Madame, than could be had by winning at any other game. The town tolerated her because of her charm, and a gambling woman with the skill she possessed was a novelty in the Mother Lode. Dumont was well liked and held considerable respect in the community and Dumont's was an immediate success. She was always smiling.

Amongst the clattering chips and the hum of men's voices, she asked the men clustered around two dozen or more gaming tables to withhold vulgar language and from telling offensive stories in front of her. Dumont rolled her own cigarette in a haze of cigar smoke, when a man asked to buy her a glass of whiskey. She shook her head, and a whisper told him "Madame drinks only champagne," he tried again, this time offering champagne, Dumont smiled, and said, "Oui". Eleanor Dumont would drink champagne with the chosen few but never too much. If anyone ever was to get too close, she would tell them to "stay an arm length away, I'm a lady."

In consequence, her clientele behaved civilized, more calm than in any other establishment in town. Dumont befriended a handsome, well-mannered gambler in his late twenties by the name of Lucky Dave Tobin. After hours, the duo would dream of expanding and opening an establishment together. He had recognized her entrepreneurial skills and to all appearances, he seemed honest. Another competent dealer would allow her to increase the business. Eventually, Dumont and Tobin moved forward with opening a new establishment together. Tobin had tried to get romantic with Eleanor, but she considered their relationship strictly platonic. Eleanor had her eye on someone else.

E.G. Waite, the editor of the Nevada Journal, sat down at his desk. He looked at the envelope sent from the attractive Eleanor Dumont. Inside, there was an invitation to the grand opening of the "Vingt-Et-Un" on Broad Street and the printing order for a new handbill which advertised the opening of the best gambling emporium in northern California. Eleanor was personally inviting him to enjoy a game with her, with free champagne for all.He so far had ignored all of her advances. *Vingt-Et-Un* had opened. The establishment would only allow well-behaved and well-groomed men.

Gas chandeliers, carpets, fine furnishings, and a dozen games day and night. Tobin managed the faro, keno, and other large games, and Dumont drew the men in, in droves and handled the smaller games like vingt-et-un. Her table was by far the most popular in the place, and she continued her habit of treating her patrons fairly and never hesitating to loan or give them money if they needed it. The mesmerizing Eleanor Dumont earned the title as the "Blackjack Queen of the Northern Mines".

Dumont continued pursuing E.G. Waite, the editor of the Nevada Journal and Waite continued to refuse her affections. Dumont was devastated. She gave up on love and turned to alcohol. Eventually, Dumont wore down and fell prey to Lucky Tobin. Dumont and Tobin continued their partnership for about eighteen months, during which time business receipts doubled, then tripled. Tobin wanted a larger share of the take, and Eleanor refused. Tobin was no gentleman, in fact he was an abusive man. Lucky Tobin beat Dumont and tried with no avail to take over the gambling parlor.

As her novelty as a lady card dealer began to wear off, surface gravel had increased rapidly and miners began to leave Nevada City. Eleanore Dumont came to her senses and finally left him, continuing the operation alone. Tobin left town. Madame Dumont stacked money for two months after Tobin's departure, she too packed up her cards. She arrived in Nevada City unannounced, and disappeared into the night in the same fashion. Dumont wandered from mining camp to mining camp. She gambled, saved money, and kept an eye out for Dave Tobin.

Dumont ended up gambling in Murphys, California. The town was established by Irish Daniel Murphy, a member of the Stephens-Townsend-Murphy group, the first immigrant party to successfully bring wagons over the Sierra in 1844.

Buildings bearing thick stone walls, iron shutters, and pastoral gardens with white picket fences lined the street. The fortunes found in the town attracted adventure seekers, gamblers, opportunists, ladies of easy virtue, and honest men, as well as Mark Twain, Joaquin Murietta and Black Bart. After her short stay, Dumont stood in the smashed up saloon in the early hours of the morning. Stepping over smashed bottles and broken chairs, she knelt down to a sleeping miner to relieve the drunk of the gold purse that laid near him. Her new whip friend Slim was gone. He had evaporated like a cheap perfume. She had planned to leave town with him in his Concord Stagecoach.

That was when a man quietly stepped behind her, grabbing her waist. Without fear, she turned to face the man. She traveled with two cousins, both derringers and the one whom she called Clyde was quickly placed against his temple. “You try anything and you will have three eyes”. Moving behind the bar that was lit only by the rising sun beaming through the slats in the wall, she poured herself a glass of champagne, and flipped a coin. Colorado or the Comstock?

Dumont took her winnings to Carson City, Nevada to buy a ranch. Dumont planned to settle down and retire from gambling. She fell in love with her land, and spent all of her time there. She spent everything she had saved improving her dream property. Jack McKnight introduced himself to Eleanor in Carson City, Nevada. He told her of his success in the cattle business. Jack McKnight gave every impression of being a wealthy and successful man. They began spending time together on Dumont’s ranch and McKnight won Dumont’s affections. Eleanor fell in love, and put her trust in Jack.

Quickly, McKnight used Dumont’s capital and bought a cattle ranch, just outside of Carson City, Nevada. A few months later, Jack’s true intentions were realized when he cleaned out Dumont’s bank account, sold the ranch, stole her jewelry, and deserted her. Eleanor wasn't the type to take this kind of treatment lying down. Dumont gave herself a moment to feel sorry for herself. Just a moment, and then quickly set off to find McKnight's. She found him a day's ride away on the trail, and rekindled their acquaintance with the aid of a double barreled shotgun. Gifting her ex the contents of both barrels straight in the chest at close range. Saying goodbye to the man who had broken her heart.

Dumont never got her money back, but she got her revenge. McKnight's bullet ridden body was found but his death was not investigated. Dumont denied responsibility, but claimed her joy that McKnight was indeed dead. Dumont was penniless and on her own. She began to drink even more. The obvious solution was to return to the only profession she knew, dealing cards. For the next five years, the insatiable Madame wandered from boom town to boom town, rarely staying long in one place. She rebuilt her purse, continuing her lifelong habit of generously treating the losers as she collected her winnings.

The placer mines out west were vanishing. Prospectors were leaving California and Colorado, and many headed for Montana territory. Dumont followed. Eleanor Dumont found her way to the new camp of Bannack, Montana. There, she opened a new gambling parlor. The baby fuzz on her lip had now developed into a growth of unusual proportions for a woman. A disgruntled miner who'd lost his temper and a bundle at her table gave her the name "Madame Moustache".

The thin, pretty girl of San Francisco of 1849 was now a more heavy character who sat in the chair, rather than standing at the blackjack table. In Bannack Montana, on a dusty alley on a dark night, Eleanor was walking home alone after a long shift. Out of the shadows, two large men lurched at the woman and trapped her against a wall made up of wooden planks. A scruffy face pressed against hers. He reeked of whiskey. "Give me all yer earnings, or else." Eleanor, as calm as could be, made eyes with the drunk man and his sleazy friend. "Oh boys," she whispered as she enticingly started to raise her skirt. "I cannot give you my purse, though you may partake in something else, if you please." Riveted, the criminals gawked at Eleanor's under garments as they were gradually exposed. With one hand, from beneath her skirt, Eleanor Dumont pulled out her Derringer, and fired it point blank in the drunken man's chest, and he dropped where he stood. His friend quickly disappeared back into the shadows from where he came, and the man on the ground never moved again. It was time to move.

Dumont found her way to the prosperous yet rowdy town of Fort Benton, Montana. Front Street was packed with brothels, saloons, dance halls and gambling houses. The cross streets of 15th and 16th Streets was known as "the bloodiest block in the West". Madame Moustache set up a table there in a gambling house the locals called "The Jungle". She began to make a name for herself. Rumors around town spoke of the steamboat Walter B. Dance, which had been heard to be a "smallpox carrier".

One night, as Dumont was dealing cards, Walter B. Dance was heading up the Missouri River. Dumont spotted the steamboat and stormed out to the river, mud at her feet. The captain stood on the deck, and while looking to the shoreline he saw Dumont storming to the river's edge with two pistols. She was screaming. He was not welcome there. By threatening the captain of the boat she very well may have saved the flourishing town's community from suffering many deaths. Not all boats were turned away.

The Missouri River sternwheeler steamboat officer Louis Rosche docked at a raucous waterfront town that same week. He stepped ashore. The man wasn't a gambler, he worked too hard for the money he made. Although he had saved up a couple hundred dollars and was curious enough to try his hand at Madame Moustache's table. Maybe he would be lucky and win enough to buy an interest in his own steamboat. Louis entered the weather-beaten, two-story frame gambling hall. The bar and gaming tables were housed in one big foggy downstairs room, slapping cards and clicking dice greeting his ears. Smoke, whiskey and sweat stung his nose. The interior was in worse wear than the outside, with a filthy floor and a dilapidated bar running along the wall. The spittoons on the floor seemed useless, for the customers were remarkably bad marksmen. The sound of clinking glasses and shuffling cards suddenly died down. The door had swung open. He glanced quickly towards the door to see a woman entering the room. She wore a black silk dress that went high around her neck.

"If I had not seen the unbelievable black brush on the woman's upper lip, I would not have known that this was the famous Madame Moustache."

The Madame sat herself in the center of the room and began shuffling the cards. The rings on her fingers glittering in the lamplight. Rosche approached her, and emptied his poke on her table. "Ma'am, there's more than $200 there. Let's get going now, and I don't want to quit until you've got all my money or until I've got a considerable amount of yours." "Oui, it shall be vingt-et-un." The heavy, sweet scent of Miss Dumont's tobacco was making him feel light-headed.

"It would be painful to exhume the memories of the hour that followed. When it was all over and my bills and gold and silver pieces were stacked neatly in front of the Madame, I got up quickly, returned my empty leather purse to my pocket, and started to leave." Dumont waved her hands excitedly. "No, no, no! The steamboat-man must not go before he has had his drink on the house," the barkeeper slammed a glass of warm milk down on the dirty table.

Madame Mustache soon followed the rush to the Black Hills to Deadwood, South Dakota. At the edge of town, she practiced her aim with her new frontierswoman friend, Martha Canary. Martha coached Eleanor in trade after an afternoon of lessons of 21. Dumont attempted to teach the cowgirl the finer points of playing. Martha, better known as Calamity Jane, never developed the talent for cards that Madame Moustache had, but Madame Moustache was a pretty good shot. While in Tombstone, Eleanor Dumont made friends with Big Nose Kate, and her longtime partner, the Sheriff of Tombstone, Wyatt Earp, his brother, and Doc Holliday. Wyatt and Holliday were then famous for their role in the gunfight at the OK Corral.

She soon made her way to the richest silver mine area discovered in the United States, a thriving silver boom town founded in 1877, once called Goose Flats. When Dumont arrived in the town, they were calling it Tombstone, Arizona. In Tombstone, Dumont saw that more income was to be made from prostitution that from playing cards. The Brothel known as Blond Marie's business was booming and Eleanor decided to open up a rival house just down the street. She hired a variety of girls, who worked day and night just down the way from the Bird Cage, the largest theatre in Tombstone. No self respecting woman would even walk on the same side of the street as the Bird Cage Theatre, but men would start their night there, Scantily dressed women would dance and entertain in cage-like structures hung from the ceilings, the men then finished the night at Blond Marie's or Dumont's.

Dumont worked up a bitter rivalry with Blond Marie, the rival working girls and the more pure ladies in town, who looked down upon Dumont and her painted ladies. Eleanor was unfazed, and in fact enjoyed ruffling their petticoats. On Sundays Dumont had her ladies put on their best dresses, and loaded them into an open wagon. A sugar cube-size emerald flashed on the hand holding her cigar, as Madame Moustache drove up and down the streets of Tombstone, giving the men a good look at her inventory. They would all be sure to wave at the finer ladies in town as they stared back at the stage in disgust. She would tell them, "A ripe beauty needs to be a step ahead of all men and their smoking six-shooters, before she's not so ripe."

Dumont eventually found herself back in San Francisco. It was the perfect place to master her strategy. She opened yet another gambling palace, this one more opulent than the previous. The marble ballroom dripped in french aesthetic, accented with mahogany detail, fluffy pink pillows, imported french plate glass mirrors. She only hired french girls, and dressed them in satin Parisian gowns and braided tiny white flowers into their hair.

Lotta Crabtree, Vaudeville's gift to the West, was performing while Dumont was living in the city. Dumont rented a private theatre box. Lotta portrayed six different characters in the first act during her set of The Little Detective. Lotta followed the act with her rendition of her mentor, Lola Montez's signature spider dance. Eleanor gasped and yelped as Lotta stomped each eight legged creature away, a piece of clothing, tearing off with each defeated Spider. Dumont was thoroughly impressed.

Dumont went home that evening after the show and gushed over the spectacular Lotta Crabtree to her working girls. Dumont was fascinated with Lotta, like many women of the time. Inspired by the young star, Dumont had all of her working girls dance down. Commercial Street the following evening, wearing only sunflowers and daffodils, dropping most of the flowers at the feet of stupefied policemen. That September, in a real estate circular, Dumont read that Miss Crabtree, before leaving California, purchased a lot on the south-side of Turk Street, east of Hyde. Dumont hired a carriage that instant and by the end of the day, purchased 96 acres of land in Contra Costa County "for when I grow old" she promised herself.

Just east of the Sierra Nevada Mountain range the short lived gold mining town of Bodie was known as "a sea of sin, lashed by the tempests of lust and passion". Bill Body found gold there in 1859. The following winter, Body was caught outside his cabin by a snowstorm and froze to death. Coyotes stripped his flesh before his partner found him in the spring. The first load of Bodie ore at the Bodie Mining Co. weighed in at over 10,000 lbs.

A young girl was praying the night before her family left to try their hand at fate, the suggestive termination of a sweet little three year old's prayer was "Goodbye God, I'm going to Bodie in the morning". Robberies, stage hold ups, and street fights made life exciting for Bodie residents. Killings happened on a daily basis. It was said that, "A Bodie man never has two disputes with the same man because he had already killed him at the first quarrel."

In May 1878, Dumont decided to see what all the fuss was about, boarding the non-stop stage from Carson City, arriving in the town of eight thousand, where the main street was over a mile long. Her arrival was such an event, even the local newspaper acknowledged the coming of the famous gambler. The townspeople welcomed her with open arms.

The paper reported "Madame Moustache, whose real name is Eleanor Dumont, has settled for the time in Bodie, following her old avocation of dealing twenty-one as force of circumstances seem to demand. Probably no woman on the Coast is better known." That winter, a man was cut to pieces in Bodie, the Gold Hill News queried, "Why can't a man get along in Bodie without fighting?" Bodie's press answered whimsically, blaming the district's 8,500-foot elevation. "Really, we can't say. It must be the altitude. There is some irresistible power in Bodie which impels us to cut and shoot each other." The clashing of revolvers up and down Main Street can be constantly heard, and a man cannot go to his dinner without getting a bullet hole in his hat, or the seat of his unmentionables cut away by the deadly knife of the desperado. Yes, it is sad, but only too true, that everybody must fight that comes to Bodie.

For over a year, in smoke filled saloons with abundant liquor, Eleanor spent long nights dealing cards, rubbing shoulders with the prominent members of Bodie. She shared afternoon walks through Bodie's Chinatown which ran at a right angle to Bodie's Main Street with her new friend Lottie Johl. Lottie had begun her time in Bodie as a sex worker, eventually marrying a German man who had set up the Union Market Butcher Shop. Lottie's past working in the red light district caused many people to shun her, but not the Madame Moustache. They strolled unbothered among the several hundred Chinese residents, Opium dens and their Taoist temple. Dumont made a quiet living in Bodie, but was never able to replace the fortune taken from her by Jack McKnight.

Eleanor had been spiraling emotionally downward for months. One tragic evening, on the corner of Union and Main, she lost everything she had in a game that evening. The honest woman borrowed three hundred dollars to stake in a card game from a new friend. It lasted only a few hours, and the Madame could not pay her back. After all her years of generosity, there was no one left willing to lend Eleanor a stake.

At the Saloon where her table had been for the past year, she rose and ordered a glass of milk, and a bottle of red wine. She sipped on the glass as she said a quiet goodnight to the men there and headed out the door. Eleanor went to her room at the Bon-Ton Lodging House and sat down on the wooden table at the edge of the bed. She scribbled a short note. "I am tired of life," and indicated her wishes for the disposition of her few possessions.

Dumont then took a bottle off the table, and left the hotel. She walked down the street and out of town, into the desert. A sheep herder found her body the next morning, next to an empty morphine vial with a bouquet of poppies and the hastily scribbled note still clutched in her hand, a rock for a pillow beneath her head. Broke and all alone, amongst the sagebrush and the lonely howls of the coyote, Eleanor Dumont Madame Moustache ended her life on October 7, 1880.

The Bodie Standard News from Oct. 9, 1880 read "Last Monday, the dead body of a woman was found about 2 miles south of Bodie on the road leading to

Bridgeport. The body was identified as that of Madam Dumont, familiarly known as "Madam Mustache" in almost every mining camp from Utah and Idaho to California. She was a French woman, very quiet and inoffensive, but with a very strong propensity for gambling. Her favorite game was "21" which she has dealt for many years. For 21 years, she has been a familiar character to the shifting population of the mining camps."

Word of her death spread like wildfire throughout the towns of the West. The citizens of Bodie passed the hat around to collect money to send her off properly, and men travelled hundreds of miles to attend her funeral. The gamblers of the place buried her with all honors, Men from all over the West joined the procession and retired to the saloons to raise a glass in her honor. It is said that of the hundreds of funerals held in the mining camp, that of 'Madame Moustache' was the largest. So many carriages were needed for the funeral procession, carriages were brought to be used in the funeral cortege from Carson City, a distance of 120 miles.

Eleanor Dumont was laid to rest in the Bodie cemetery where she resides to this day, among gunmen, illegitimate children, prostitutes, split-rail fences and beautiful ironwork. The lonely fences, like the frames of vacant beds, punctuate the sagebrush covered hills and underscore the vast, silent isolation of the dead who've been left behind. Although the marker on her grave has long since disappeared and now no one is quite sure of exactly where it rests.

If you visit the state park mining town of Bodie, do not take a thing. If you do, legend says that you will be cursed with bad luck until the item is returned. Many people have tried taking things from the town, and they have all returned the items due to the bad luck they endured. Catherine Jones, the park interpreter, said, "Pretty much every time the ranger goes to the post office to pick up our mail, there's a cursed artifact in there." The team has now received so many of these letters over the years that they're now collected, on display, in the Bodie museum. One of the ominous letters, received in 2002, reads:

"Fair warning for anyone that thinks this is just folklore -- my life has never seen such turmoil. Please take my warning and do not remove even a speck of dust."

Highsmith, Carol M, photographer. *Bodie is a ghost town in the Bodie Hills east of the Sierra Nevada Mountain range in Mono County, California*. United States California Bodie, 2012. Photograph. https://www.loc.gov/item/2013632798/

Surrender
17

Wherever you are in this hemisphere, you are on Native land. Never forget that before the Spanish arrived in California, for thousands of years, from sea to shining sea, this was Indian country. More than 300,000 Natives lived here, representing more than 100 tribes, each with its individual traditions and cultures, most completely lost by the arrival of settlers. Never forget that Russian and European and American colonists, and Spanish missionaries' arrival on the Pacific coastline forever changed the native people's way of life. Write that down, and burn it into your brain.

The first known interaction with the Natives in California was in the Monterey area in 1602, when Sebastián de Vizcaíno's Spanish expedition was searching for a safe harbor for their ships. Well-over 100 years then passed with little attention paid to Alta California. Then, Gaspar de Portola's expedition of Spanish missionaries arrived in the Monterey area in 1769 and Spain began colonizing. Erasing the identities of the California indigenous people who entered the missions.

The San Rafael Mission was established, removing Pomo people from their lands, bringing them to the new mission. They were given a wool shirt with long sleeves called a cotón, and a wool blanket. The women were also given a wool petticoat and men received a breechclout to cover their groin area. They were then forcibly baptized into the Catholic faith, and thrown into labor camps that were filthy and disease ridden. Five years down the road, California became part of the Mexican Republic, and the Mexican government gave out large tracts of Pomo land to its settlers. The foreign white colonists brought deadly diseases and epidemics.

In one instance, a Russian ship brought a case of smallpox, the indigenous people did not have immunity to such diseases, the tribe populations heavily decreased. The bones of thousands "left unburied, bleached the hills" of Sonoma and Napa counties. As all this happened, the domestic stock animals brought by the foreigners damaged the gathering areas while they grazed and consumed all of the native foods. Stream channels were disturbed and often re-routed, land was blasted away and huge amounts of soil entered streams and rivers, destroying the habitat of fish and other aquatic species that the indigenous people depended on for survival. Ten years later there was a massive malaria outbreak. The following year the missions were authorized by the crown to "convert" all of the Natives within a ten-year period. They had until 1844. They were to surrender their control over the mission's livestock, fields, orchards and buildings to the Indians in 1844. The padres never achieved their goal and the lands and wealth were then stolen from the Natives. The California Mission System was not the sugar cube fantasy we were fed in fourth grade. Debunked. Unpack that. Accept it.

A hero of mine, Benjamin Madley, is an associate professor of history at UCLA and has been on a more than decade-long odyssey to document and reveal the existence of this government sponsored genocide. He said, "The history of genocide casts a shadow over California. It hovers over the land of the endless summer, over Disneyland, over the surfers, the Beach Boys, the palm trees, the Hollywood Sign… and yet, there is also a story of California Indian resistance and survival that is miraculous."

Lawrence & Houseworth, Publisher. *Group of Digger Indian Squaws.* 1866. [Published] Photograph. https://www.loc.gov/item/2002723574/

Survival

18

The wilderness holds an abundance of power. Power that is manifested in the rocks, the springs, the animals, and the trees. A Power that is sought after and/or found when stumbled upon. The indigenous people of the Americas are familiar with this power. The foreigners who came to this land usually did not refer to the natural beauty and the magic it held, but the wealth it retained.

An Eastern Pomo woman ponders over petroglyphs on the face of boulders near her village of Danoha in Clearlake, California. Her family had lived here for thousands of years. The petroglyphs, at the entrance of a natural tunnel in a collection of boulders, were known as the baby rocks. She has fasted for four days, and she has come alone, seeking to move through the rocks, in an altered state of consciousness. The baby rocks held the spirits of the future children to be born to the parents who followed this Pomo ritual. There was a power affecting fertility there. The carved petroglyphs allowed her entrance, where she negotiated with Mother Earth. Nine months later, Ni'ka was born in the village of Danoha, under the sod roof of her family's dome-shaped home made of tule and earth covered wooden poles.

It was 1849. Ni'ka sat with her mother, watching her making a basket with great care, weaving in the Dau, or Spirit Door. This Spirit Door would allow good spirits to come and circulate inside of the basket while the good or bad spirits were released. The base of the basket was completely covered in vivid red feathers of the pileated woodpecker, the surface so smooth, it resembled the breast of the bird itself.

Her mother had a sacred gift in making the baskets the family used for cooking, storing food, their religious ceremonies, and daily life. Her technique was exquisite. Together, they collected basket materials annually, swamp canes, rye grass, black ash, willow shoots, sedge roots, the bark of redbud, the root of bulrush, and the root of the gray pine.

Ni'ka's mother taught the five year old girl everything she knew when it came to drying, cleaning, splitting, soaking, and dying the materials. It would be many weeks before the basket was finished. In the coming weeks, she would be taught to fasten beads to the basket's border and the pendants of abalone shell Ni'ka had worked to polish would be attached. In the distance, she could see the fellow children in her tribe arriving home from their gathering expeditions on the outside. The community and culture was the "inside" of their home, and the wilderness and wild areas to which they went for hunting and gathering wild foods was the "outside."

A dualism, a contrast of community and wilderness, domestic and wild, culture and nature. Surely their baskets would be filled with bulbs, roots, clover, pinole seeds, gooseberries, blueberries, raspberries, blackberries, wild greens, gnats, mushrooms, acorns, nuts, caterpillars, grasshoppers and Yerba Buena. The men in the tribe were away on a hunt with bows and harpoons, in search of deer, elk, antelope, rabbit, sea lions, rats, squirrels, waterfowl, and birds. They would periodically burn the land to remove hiding places for the game. They would also fish for salmon, carp, blackfish, clams and mussels.

Women gave life, and because the giving of life was a woman's most important role, she did not participate in the taking of life, which included coming in contact with weapons. Instead, the women worked at home, gathering food and materials and preparing the plant based foods. They would shell the acorns, crushing and watering them till they were easy to work with. Next, they would ground the acorns into a paste or to make mush, bread, and soup. Pies would be made with the acorn meal and gathered berries and nuts. Ni'ka enjoyed her life on the inside and was unaware of the struggles of the nearby Pomo tribes, and Ni'ka was unaware of what this meant for her, her family, her tribe, and her cherished land.

Ninety miles north of San Francisco in Clearlake, 15,000 cattle and 2,500 horses lived on Big Valley Ranch. Salvador Vallejo had sold the property in 1847 to Andrew Kelsey and Charles Stone, the first Anglo-American colonists in the Clear Lake region. Andrew Kelsey and his three brothers had hoisted the Bear Flag with the Bear Flag Party in Sonoma in 1846. They were rough and often in trouble with the authorities. On their ranch, they made the rules.

Raiding the surrounding Eastern Pomo and Wapo villages, Stone and Kelsey and Co. captured several hundred Native Pomo and Wapo people. They forced their slaves to construct and operate their empire. Everything was taken from the natives, including fishing supplies, and simple knives. The men were used as vaqueros, which in English translates to cattle drivers or cowboys.

The vaqueros were forced into back breaking labor as they dug wells and built the grand hacienda, outbuildings and a barrier in which they would remain inside, along with their wives and children. Imprisoned. Behind the high fence, for their own entertainment, Andrew Kelsey and Charles Stone brutally mistreated the Natives. Disrespectfully, they called them "Diggers". The often drunken white men shot at the Wapo and Pomo for the fun of seeing them jump. Kelsey and Stone had taken local Pomo Chief Augustine's wife as a sex slave and constantly ordered Pomo fathers to bring them their daughters to be sexually used and abused, and the men who resisted were whipped, lashed and hung by the hands or toes. This was a usual punishment and it occurred at least two or three times a week.

If a worker broke any rule, they would be hung "up by his thumbs, so that his toes just touched the floor, and keep him there for two or three days, sometimes with nothing to eat." Andrew Kelsey and Charles Stone ruled over the Eastern Pomo and Clear Lake Wapo people using fear, torture, sadism, and murderous force for many years. The enslaved Pomo people were nearly starved. Kelsey and Stone hardly provided food and had banned them from foraging, hunting and fishing on their land.

Eighteen of the main herdsmen and their two foreman were the only Slaves being fed. The men would receive about six pints of boiled wheat each for a day's work, and the men would share the wheat back at home, so these herders were also starving. The people were getting restless. Twenty elders had died from starvation over winter and four of the Native slaves had been killed by severe whipping in the early months of 1849.

"The inside" was no longer safe. Da-Pi-Tauo was sick and starving. She was the wife of Big Jim, a native Pomo slave at Big Valley Ranch. Da-Pi-Tauo's sister who was the wife of Shuk, an 18 year old Pomo man. Shuk would later become the Hoolanapo Pomo chief Augustine. She was now Stone's personal slave.Da-Pi-Tauo sent her son to her sister. "Tell your aunt that I am starving and sick, ask for a handful of wheat." He hurried to Stone's house and told his aunt just what his mother had said. His aunt, fearful for her sister's health, gave her nephew 5 cups of wheat that she tied it up in an apron of hers.

The young man started for the camp with the precious gift in a hurry to help his sick mother. Stone spotted the boy running from the house and called him back. Stone approached the boy and swatted the wheat from his hands. The apron fell to the ground, wind blowing the grains away. The young boy tried to gather the life saving substance but was captured by Stone and taken to a nearby tree, where he was tied up and given 100 lashes. When Stone had enough, he shot the young boy.

Da-Pi-Tauo's son suffered for two whole days before he died, his punishment for attempting to feed his starving mother. Action had to be taken by the natives or all would be lost. It was decided that Shuk and Xasis, the head-riders of the eighteen herdsmen, would be secretly hired to kill a cow and bring it back to the village. The people had to eat.

The foreman debated the plan all night, night or day, and the order of action, deciding by the end, to do the job at night. They would take the best lasso horses in the barn. The best lasso horses in the barn, of course, belonged to Stone and Kelsey. Shuk promised, Somebody" is going to get killed on this job."

Under the moonlight from a cloudy sky, Shuk and Xasis crept to the house to see if Kelsey and Stone had gone to bed. They had. It was drizzling on them as they went to the barn and took their horses and saddles. The plan was to round up the band that was feeding out west. Shuk would make the first lasso and Xasis would do the foot lassing.

Under the stars, Shuk called out, "I see a big one here, hurry and come on!" Shuk saw his chance and threw the rope on a hefty ox. As Xasis rushed over, the stampede began. The ox joined in. Shuk's horse was pulled to the wet, slippery ground, he was knocked off, and the horse and the ox got away. Basis attempted to get his rope on, but was too far away, and eventually, he gave up the chase. Defeated, Xasis returned Kelsey's horse to the barn. The bad news was reported to the men of the tribe who had gathered in Xasis's house. They all knew death was in the pot for Shuk and Xasis.

The men faced another night of debate. It seemed obvious to Shuk and Xasis that the solution was to kill the white men. No one agreed. A Wapo man offered the suggestion of the tribe giving Stone and Kelsey forty sticks of beads, the equivalent of 16,000 beads or one hundred dollars. Thirty-six hundred dollars in 2022. No one agreed. One of the men thought they could tell Stone or Kelsey the horse was stolen. No one agreed. Another man suggested that the other horse should be turned out and that they tell Stone and Kelsey both horses were stolen. No one agreed. It was not looking good for Shuk and Xasis, and the men decided murder was the only option.

Starvation was the main reason the slaves at Big Valley Ranch wanted Stone and Kelsey dead, but hardly the only motive. They set out together, that early December morning of 1849 to save their people. To do right and fear no man. A man known as Busi decided to join the men as daylight was approaching. The boys and girls of the village worked inside the household as servants. Kra-nas and Ma-Laxa-Qe-Tu joined the band when, in the wee hours, the children worked together to remove every gun, knife, bow and arrow and anything that could be used as a weapon from the home.

Da-Pi-Tauo's sister poured water onto the two men's gunpowder, rendering it useless. Kelsey and Stone would be helpless in defense.

Charles Stone would start each morning all alone, boiling wheat for the 18 herdsmen and their two foremen. This morning, when Stone showed up carrying a pot from the fireplace, he was shocked to see five of the men already waiting for him. He was curious.

"What's the matter, boys? You came early this morning. Something wrong?" Busi responded, "Oh nothing, me hungry that's all." Kra-nas looked confused and said to Shuk, "I thought we came to kill this man? Give me these arrows and bows." Kra-nas pulled the bow and the arrow from Shuk's hands and pointed right at Stone. Stone whispered "What are you trying to do?" as the arrow was cut loose, striking him in the stomach.

Stone pulled the arrow out of his torso and attempted to take off running towards the house. The men surrounded him and they began to throw blows. Busi's arm was broken after Stone struck him with the fire pot, and he succeeded in getting into the house, locking the door behind him. Kelsey soon arrived, noticing blood on the doorstep of Stone's home.

The men jumped out to ambush him and a fight ensued, Kelsey said to the men. "Don't kill Kelsey, Kelsey good man for you." Kranas replied, "Yes, you are such a good man that you have killed many of us." Kelsey broke free and ran for the creek, but not before he was shot in the back with two arrows.

As he approached the creek, Kelsey managed to pull the arrows out before he dove into the water, staying out of sight until approaching the opposite shore. Where, surprise, several Native men were waiting for him. One of the men was Ju-Luh, a man Kelsey knew well. He begged Ju-Luh for his life, as he lost blood, and became weak. Ju-Luh said, "It's too late Kelsey; if I attempt to save you. I also will be killed. I cannot save you." Ju-Luh and Big Jim held Kelsey by the arms and took him to his wife, Da-Pi-Tauo.

"This is a man who killed our son, take this spear." Da-Pi-Tauo stabbed the white man in the heart and his body was left for the coyotes. At the house, Xasis and Qra-Nas were chasing a breathless Stone, following the drops of blood. The trail led the men to a door, where Stone's foot revealed his location, crawling up the stairs. Qra-Nas drew his arrow across the bow and Xasis swung the door open but Stone did not move. He had bled to death, or so they thought. They took his body, and threw it out the window.

Somehow, Stone got back up and ran to the forest, where Da-Pi-Tauo's sister found him and used a rock to end his life for good. The woman who was taken from her home and forced to be the sex slave to the men, was the final hand in both their fates. The group reunited at the house, and immediately gathered food to bring home to their families. The men who were able to ride, took a horse and left for the valleys and upper lake to hunt. There were thousands of cattle and they would eat well. The women of the tribes went to the house and gathered all the corn and wheat they could pack up. The plan was for the women, children and elders to flee to hiding places at Scotts Valley and Fishels Point. The men would stay behind to keep watch.

John W. Davidson, Virginian, was preparing himself to sit down for a Christmas dinner with his family. On the table, oyster and chestnut stuffing and a large wild turkey were waiting on the table, filling the home with the most delicious scent. His children rushed to the table, excited to eat the beautiful meal. There was a knock at the door, the Davidson family was not expecting visitors on this holiday evening. At the door, stood a rider carrying a post for the First Lieutenant.

The post carried the news that Charles Stone and Andrew Kelsey of Clear Lake had been murdered by some of the Native Pomo men that they were holding in captivity. John Davidson sat down at the table, staring at the letter, forgetting about the turkey and oyster and chestnut stuffing. Davidson knew Andrew Kelsey from his association with the US Army Captain John C. Frémont during the initial US invasion of the territory that would soon be called California.

General Smith of the First Dragoons believed in collective punishment. Smith declared that, "As soon as troops can move in the spring, the California Indians who committed the murder on Clear Lake must be chastised." Someone would pay for this. On the afternoon of the day after Christmas, twelve hours had passed since Davidson had received the news of Kelsey and Stone's passing. Lieutenant Nathaniel Lyon was getting ready to begin a seventy mile journey north.

Lieutenant Lyon led a detachment of 22 men from a regiment of the US Army's First Dragoons. For three long days, the militia of determined white men moved through dense brush and grasses that were nearly as tall as them. The men were rowdy and often drunk as they rode through hills of towering oak trees, making their way to Clear Lake. The mission was retaliation against the Native Pomo People, and the white men's hearts were set on extermination.

Just south of Calistoga, Clear Lake Wappo women and men were going about their daily life inside their large village. When they woke up that morning, they had no reason to think that it was not just another typical day, unsuspecting of an approaching cavalry. On a typical day of battle for brave Wappo men, Wappo warriors would have painted themselves with black, red, and white paint. Large bird wings would be worn in their hair. Yet they were left surprised, when Lyon and his men bombarded the village, killing thirty-five

Wappo people with their open fire. Eleven Natives of all ages were murdered as they innocently walked out of their sweat house, their bodies then burned in their homes. Then they just left.

The posse headed for the Cyrus family ranch to recruit more men to join in on the battle ahead. At the Cyrus ranch, the soldiers attempted to north the settlers to help them rid the area of Natives. The locals absolutely refused. The labor of the California Indians was depended on by the farmers.

One man declared, "If we treat them kindly and pay them fairly, they are quite pleasant."

Defeated, the band of vigilantes left, they would handle the job by themselves. For weeks, the posse chased after and promised to kill every California Indian they found as they passed through Sonoma. Simultaneously Benjamin Kelsey, was burning more Rancherias and chasing men to their death. The Napa locals were combative to the posse's violence and requested help from the Governor.

As they waited, they banded together to turn back the cavalry in Napa, crushing the plans to cross on the ferry. North of St. Helena, there was a large Rancheria belonging to more men of the Bear Flag Revolt, Henry Fowler and William Hargrave. The militia intruded upon the Rancheria, and burned their lodges and sacred spaces. They shot at least 15 of the local Wappo people and before they abandoned the scene, they sabotaged the survivors' supply of barley and wheat. Leaving the bodies of the slain children, women and men in their wake. The Rancheria is now known as "Human Flesh Ranch".

Shuk and Xasis patrolled the trail on the west-side of the valley. Qra-Nas and Ma-Laq-Qe-Tou were chosen to watch the trail that came in from the lower lake, and Yom-mey-nah and Ge-we-leh were watching the trail that came from Eight Mile Valley. For two weeks, no white person was seen on the trail until two on horseback coming over the hill from the lower lake were spotted by Qra-nas and Ma-Laq-Qe-Tou. The men, even from a far distance, noticed the camp was deserted. The white men noticed Qra-nas and Ma-Laq-Qe-Tou coming towards them and they took off.

Another three days passed, and no one was seen. Two Pomo men were camped at the top of the North peak of Uncle Sam Mountain, watching for danger for four days, when early one morning, a long boat with a pole on the bow with red cloth was seen, and it was followed by several more, and each boat held ten to fifteen men. Watching the trail from Ash Hill, the two men saw the infantries coming over the hill. The men were marching, firing shots with threatening guns. A smoke signal was sent and a tule canoe was spotted by the lake watchers, "Some news coming." They needed to hide. They retreated to leave for Oregon.

Kelsey had a brother, Benjamin, and he was looking for revenge. Benjamin Kelsey rounded up a posse. The posse was a militia led by Lieutenant Nathaniel Lyon and Lieutenant John W. Davidson including the Cavalry detachment of the US First Dragoons Regiment. They made a plan. A random campaign of violence against all Clear Lake Pomo had been waged. They men went to Stone and Kelsey's house, and then down towards the lake. They moved across the valley near the lake port, Scotts Valley, to the upper lake to set up camp on Emerson Hill.

It was there they saw the Pomo camp on the island Bo-no-po-ti. The cavalry was told that six hundred Pomo armed warriors were stationed on the island. In fact, the Pomo at Bo-no-po-ti never worked on Stone and Kelsey's ranch, and had nothing to do with their murders. The island was mostly populated with women and children, and it was where Ni'ka, and her mother were finishing up their basket.

It had been a cold winter. Staying warm inside her tule kotka by the small fire, Nika learned to make clothing from the tule, and spent hours assembling jewelry made of what was left of last season's collected abalone and clamshells. Ni'ka's mother was also teaching her daughter to sew. They were using the skin from rabbits her father had hunted, to make a blanket. The tribe members would travel to the coast to fish and gather more materials this coming summer, and Ni'kas father promised he would take her along.
Soon, he would go on a long seasonal hunting expedition with the men of the tribe and Nika would go fishing with her mother and the women and other children. Nika ran her fingers over the smooth abalone, thinking of the wonderful gifts nature bestowed on her family, anything they could ever need was right there, surrounding them in the wilderness. The now six year old Nika could not wait for the adventures to come, playing in the poppies.

"We had hoped to hear no more of Indian butcheries in California. We hope and trust the US troops in California will prevent further violence."
-Daily Alta California March 11, 1850

"Hundreds of the Indians are in the mountains in a starving condition, afraid to return to the Ranchos."
- Daily Alta California - March 19, 1850

In the chilly water that spring afternoon, the children were challenging one another in a game. With hollow tule reeds, they would lie on their backs in the shallow water, and breathe through the reed, to see who could remain underwater the longest. Ni'ka's mother took a break from her fishing to check on Ni'ka and the other children. She scanned the island for Nika and the other children, and did not see them. She looked closer, and noticed, near the tule, a collection of misplaced reeds, bobbing in the water.

She giggled to herself. This woman was incredibly pleased with her life as a parent to this young adventurous spirit. In only a few days of being on Bo-no-po-ti, Ni'ka was learning the landscape, and the power associated with it's shores, hills and rocks. To listen to the wisdom of its owl and raven calls. Studying the clouds, fog, angles of the sun and the ways of the moon in the night sky. She also learned all the many uses of tule.

The killings of the California Indians continued on the road to Bo-no-po-ti. The militia men marked their trail by hanging the men, and built large fires underneath their hanging bodies as a warning of what was still yet to come. General Smith had instructed Lyon to negotiate neither for custody of those who had killed Stone and Kelsey nor for a general surrender. Lyon, with his detachment of the Dragoons, detachment M of the 3rd Artillery, and detachments A, E, and G of the 2nd Infantry, arrived in Clear Lake. Lyon and some of his men went to observe the tribe.

Lyon saw on the island, the Natives had some natural protection on the island from the waters of Clear Lake and he sent for two small brass field guns and two whale boats from the US Army Arsenal at

Benicia. The boats were to be hauled overland, and would take some time to arrive. As they waited, locals began to volunteer themselves for the murderous expedition. When the artillery arrived, the white men moved in just two and a half miles from Bo-no-po-ti.

They set up camp at Rodman Slough on the night of May 14th. Watching from across the lake, the troops saw the people gathered on Bo-no-po-ti about three hundred yards from shore of the island. The Pomo women and a few of the men were performing in a ceremony, giving thanks for the creation of the world and for the continuation of each day. The women wore their Clam shell necklaces and dresses, and the few elder men that had stayed on the island rather than join the seasonal hunt, were in fox and deer regalia, they played the cocoon rattle, double-boned whistle, flute, plank drum, and rattle. It was a feather dance. To the white men, who witnessed this ceremony, the rhythm of the drums had so far only meant one thing to them. It sounded like a march to war.

The white men assumed the tribe were harboring those who had slain Stone and Kelsey and preparing for an epic battle. A silly assumption, at the time, for three separate languages were spoken in the four different California Indian groups lived around Clear Lake, and the Pomo from the Big Valley ranch, and the Pomo at Bo-no-po-ti, were not familiar with each other, nor did they even speak the same language. The song ended, and the Pomo people let out a loud ohhh of release at the end of their dance, startling the men who watched them.

In the dark hours of the following morning of May 15 1850, Lyon's infantrymen loaded themselves into the whale boats. Packing alongside them, cannons, their weapons, and ammunition, and they quietly crossed the water. They moved towards the northern rim of the lake, and then split and covered the north, east, and west shores of the island, positioning themselves in a crescent, patrolling the shores and closing off any route of escape in every direction.

At the break of dawn, from the south-end of the island, from his boat, Lyon opened fire on the village, followed by shots fired from the northern shore. Six year old Ni'ka and her mother were tending to the fire when they heard the first shot ring out. Nika looked at her mother with a sheer look of terror. They started to run away from the sound, to the southern shore and as they did, a cannon was fired from that direction. Panic set in, they realized they were trapped. Ge-Wi-Lih threw up his hands and tried to approach the men. "*no harm me good man"* without hesitation, Lyon shot him to death as well as the man standing next to him, the posse took the bodies to be hanged. There would be no negotiating. Women and children ran to hide and the soldiers gunned them down. Captain Lyon ordered his soldiers to follow the escaping Pomo into the thick reeds surrounding the marshy waters and "pursue and destroy as far as possible." The few elder men that remained on the island while the others were away hunting, fought back courageously, but did not last long. The brave men were captured and killed with sabers, baronets, hatchets, rocks and bare hands, one Pomo man was tied to a tree and burned alive.

When Nika and her mother approached the shore, she saw her friend with her father, one of the men who had not gone hunting. Her father was digging a large hole in a bank of the river for the two to hide in. Another friend of Nika's, who was also escaping to the water with her own mother and Nika saw them both shot and killed as they started to swim. In the shallow waters, the hunters were using sabers to take down anyone they found hiding in the tule. Captain Nathaniel Lyon said, The" island was a perfect slaughtering pen."

On the shore, Nikas mother was nearly hit by a bullet, it came so close and with a mother's instinct she dove for the water, as if hit, taking Nika down with her. She laid in the water, with Nika underneath her. For a short series of miraculous moments that played out for Nika as if in slow motion, her mother moved her hand under the water, picked a tule reed from the lake floor, and put it in Nikas hands, below the surface of the water. She whispered to her daughter. "How long can you go Ni'ka? You are good at this game. Show me."

Nika put the reed in her mouth, and went underwater. On the island, the massacre continued. Infants were being murdered by a practice used by the US soldiers and militia men of the nineteenth century. It was called "braining", the babies' heads smashed against tree trunks or under the boots of the white men. An elder woman hid under a bank covering herself with the overhanging tules. From her hiding spot, she gasped as she witnessed two white men approaching the shore, guns high in the air, on the end of their guns, a little girl hung. They threw the child's body in the water and walked away. This continued, more men approaching in the same manner, young children hanging at the ends of their weapons, their small innocent bodies, thrown into the creek.

Nika was still hidden tucked under the breast of her mother under the bloody waters. Crouching beneath the water beside the bank she sipped air through a reed to maintain her life. Her mother, acting as if she was shot dead, remained still. An eagle watched from above, then dived at a snake, ripping it to shreds.

A young boy who was a friend of Nika's, ran from the battle with his mother and siblings. Right in front of his eyes, the soldiers shot his mother and the woman fell to the ground, her tiny baby in her arms. The boy stood over his mother, shocked and scared, and his mother shooed him away, telling him in Pomo, to climb up into a tree and wait. He did.

From the high branches, he watched in disbelief, soldiers running about the camp and shooting the men and women and stabbing boys and girls. His mother was on the ground below him, dying but still not dead, continuing to tell her son to stay quiet. She laid there, holding her little baby in her arms moaning in Pomo, O my babies. She was not quite enough in her cries, and two white men heard her, came running toward the mother and baby, the young boy watched as his mother and sibling were stabbed, their bodies thrown over the bank into the water.

From the tree, he then saw a man dying, a young boy in his arms. A soldier then approached the man, finishing him off with his bayonet, and kidnapped the child. It would be known as the Bloody Island Massacre. Benjamin Madley said in his book, "An American Genocide" that, "There were not less than four hundred warriors killed and drowned at Clear Lake and as many more of squaws and children who plunged into the lake and drowned, through fear, committing suicide. So in all, about eight hundred Indians found a watery grave in Clear Lake."

Hours and hours passed since the last gunshot, and eventually, everything went quiet. No more footsteps of the soldiers, no more cries, no more gunshots. It was silent. Nika's mother opened her eyes and looked around, seeing it was all clear, she lifted Nika from under the red water. Blood was everywhere, and everyone was dead or gone.

Barefoot and bleeding, two teenage boys made the gruesome climb over Sonoma's Bottlerock Mountain, led by two US soldiers. The rocks shred the soles of their feet while the man ahead walked swiftly in his boots, and the boys tried to keep us as the man behind them stabbed at their backs with the sharp knife fixed on the end of his gun. The soldier in front noticed the native teens wincing in pain, attempting to step carefully, and stopped, instructing them to sit down. The soldier opened his pack, and took a handful of something out of a box. As he approached the boys he instructed them to put their feet up on a log in front of them, and began to rub the substance into the boys feet tying a cloth around. It was salt. The soldiers stood there laughing and the boys cried in pain.

For two hours, the men rubbed salt into the wounds where the boys had been stabbed in the back. Lieutenant Lyon's forces of US soldiers and militia men had continued throughout the area, hunting down escapees and killing any Natives they came into contact with. After three more days of captivity, the head soldier released the boys at the Lower Lake, leaving them some meat and hard bread, which the boys mostly abandoned as they ran for dear life under the impression they were being followed. The teenage boys side tracked, and climbed high peaks to scan the surrounding area for stalkers, only to run again, all the way home. The boys arrived home in hopes to see their mother and sister only to find their blood scattered over the ground like water and their bodies left for coyotes to devour. They sat under a tree and cried until dark.

A month had passed since the massacre, and Nika and mother had been surviving alone in the wilderness, in the rock crevices, caves and mountain top pools. Seeking protection from the supernatural world that surrounded them. Gathering food and medicinal plants from the holy mountains where supernatural power dwelled and visited them.

During that time, the Pomo land around the lake and beyond were taken over and homesteaded by the members of the militia, some of them prominent members of society. The Pomo survivors lived on in small bands, most living as slaves to local rancheros. The orphaned children of the murdered natives were hidden from the settlers looking for slaves. Good money was paid for such.

On April 22, 1850, just weeks before the massacre, The Act for the Government and Protection of Indians was passed. This allowed settlers to continue the California practice of capturing and using Native people as bound laborers. It provided the foundation for enslavement and trafficking within the Native American laborers, and deemed it legal to enslave and traffic its young women and children. The law allowed loitering or orphaned Native Americans found without means of support, to be claimed, and forced into labor. The Natives and Anglo Americans had opposing ideas of what were indeed "means of support". The Natives lived off the land, and had for thousands of years, and if you lived off and with the land, you did not need or want like these new foreigners. A Native person held no rights and could not testify in court, nearly every Indian in California suddenly became a candidate for slavery.

California's first governor, Peter Burnett announced that, "California was a battleground between the races and that there were only two options towards California Indians, extinction or removal, The only way we will be able to mine in security, if all of these people are exterminated." Villages were raided, supplies were stolen and women and children were kidnapped. Natives would be snatched up and charged as vagrants. When they faced the justice of the peace, they would be sold off at public auction to labor without pay for the next four months. Compensation was paid to the men who brought the Natives in for captivity, as well as payment for heads, scalps, or ears of Natives. At one time, they would earn up to twenty-five dollars for turning in a Native male body part, and five dollars for a woman or child. Millions of dollars were paid to private militias by State officials in bounties.

Legislation in California passed granting over one million dollars for the reimbursement of additional expenses that the hunters of the Natives would incur. The same legislation followed in the federal Congress allowing federal funds for the same purpose. The purpose? Genocide. Retired Sonoma State University Native American Studies Professor Edward Castillo who has written of the initial years of the California Gold Rush said, "Nothing in American Indian history is even remotely comparable to this massive orgy of theft and mass murder."

The California gold rush led Americans to rape the land and exploit its provisions and then used them towards the efforts of the extermination of those who lived here for thousands of years. It did not stop there. They exploited their women, they mistreated Asians, they exploited the Mexicans and the blacks. Sowing seeds that became the roots of a new California.

"Gold's a devilish sort of thing. You lose your sense of values and character changes entirely. Your soul stops being the same as it was before."

In the six years after the massacre, the remaining Pomo were moved onto small rancherias by the US Federal Government. This relocation was known as "Marches to Round Valley". Pomo men, women, infants and children were captured from the foothills and forced by gun and whip through the valley, crossing the Sacramento River and over by the Sutter Butte. Many had drowned in the march while crossing the river. Some escaped and remained hidden for some time, most taking on Mexican names and blending into the Mexican American communities.

Two years later in 1858, it was common to read in the newspapers the opinions and promises made by California's US Senator Jon Weller. Weller said to his colleagues that the Natives "will be exterminated before the onward march of the white man" and insisted that the "interest of white man demands their extinction".

Lieutenants Lyon and Davidson were both later promoted to Army Brigadier Generals during the Civil War, with the approval of Abraham Lincoln. Lyon became the Commander of the Department of the West, the position was previously held by John C. Frémont.

Benjamin Madley will teach you that by 1873, the number of Natives in California went from 150,000 to 30,000 due to the murders, the disease, the starvation and the dislocation. This was not a battle lost after two civilizations met and disagreed. This was genocide sanctioned and paid for by state and federal officials. There is a list of over 100 Genocidal Massacres by the United States against Indigenous Peoples of the Western Continent where accountability has never been claimed by the United States government or its military forces.
Because: EXTERMINATION WAS POLICY.

Archaeologists believe that the Clear Lake basin has been occupied by Native Americans for at least 11,000 years. Bloody Island now stands as a hilltop rising from the dusty lake bed. The Upper Lake Basin, drained and "reclaimed" for agricultural use in the 1930's. On May 20, 1942, 92 years and 5 days after the Bloody Island Massacre, the Native Sons of the Golden West installed a historical marker one-third of a mile off of U.S. Highway 20. The Native Sons were an Anglo American organization responsible for many of the placards and historical landmarks scattered throughout California. The plaque notes the site of a Battle between Cavalry under "Captain" Lyon and Indians under Chief Augustine. Right off the bat we know THAT is bullshit. It was no battle. It was a massacre. This memorial, once again, whitewashed genocide with the old "Cowboys and Indians" bit.

There are not many visitors, as this event was unmentioned in our California history textbooks. It also states the wrong date, placing the massacre on April 15, 1850, which was a month prior. The marker was desecrated in 2002, red paint was poured all over and around it. The red paint remains, left to resemble spilled blood. If you travel a quarter mile down a street called Reclamation Road, you can see the massacre site close-up.

A new plaque went up in 2005, erected by the Department of Parks and Recreation and the Lucy Moore Foundation. It gives a much more accurate history, noting it was in fact, not a battle, but rather the location where "a regiment of the 1st Dragoons of the US Cavalry, Commanded by Capt. Nathaniel Lyon and Lt. J.W. Davidson, massacred nearly the entire native population of the island." The full text of the plaque goes on to state: "Most were women and children. This act was in reprisal for the killing of Andrew Kelsey and Charles Stone who had long enslaved, brutalized, and starved indigenous people in the area."

In 2020, monuments started coming down and both sides of history began coming to light. The 1942 plaque is left up, to represent how alternate, and incorrect, versions of the past had long been told. A reminder for us as individuals, to be responsible as listeners, caretakers and creators of a shared and global historical narrative.

Every May 20th, since 1999, an annual sunrise forgiveness ceremony is held at the 1942 marker in honor, remembrance and forgiveness on behalf of the Pomo Indian People that perished and those that survived the Bloody Island Massacre. The ceremony is held not the date of the massacre, but the anniversary of when the 1942 marker was installed.

According to Nika's great-grandson, Clayton Duncan, The" ceremony is also to say we're sorry to our ancestors whose bones and ashes were shown such disrespect." It is to honor her, her prayer and all who died at Bloody Island. Candles are burned and tobacco offerings are made to the Pomo ancestors whose bodies were cremated and buried, only later to be used in the construction of dams around the Upper Lake basin.

"If we can know and learn from each other, to accept the truths of the old world and the new, perhaps our children will not see the colors of skin, the manners of our worship, our cultural heritages as characteristics that divide us," said Duncan. "Perhaps they will see them as the attributes that unite us so we can all work together to fix, mend and heal the Earth, our mother. Doing this, we know in our hearts and from the wishes of our ancestors that it will bring back the balance, using the Lucy Moore prayer of forgiveness."

"At 6 years old, she weighed not much more than one of the cannon balls that tore through the people like a boulder through willows. Crouching beneath the water beside the bank she sipped air through a reed to maintain her life. Above her, an old world was ending, washed in blood." These are the words Clayton Duncan uses to tell the story of his great-grandmother, Lucy Moore, and her survival of the events of Bloody Island.

Ni'ka, who is now better known as Lucy More, is now a hero to the Pomo people. Nika became a mother, a grandmother and great-grandmother. As an elder, her husband would play old native songs as Nika cried, telling the story to her grandchildren. She never stopped praying for her cousins, her aunts and uncles, her people. She lived to be 110 years old, and in her old age prayed every day to forgive America.

On that note....

We hold pride in the United States based on ideas of freedom. People had wanted to practice freedom of religion, and they immigrated here to do so. When they arrived, they took the natives' religion and freedoms away. It seems to me, the US was more free, Pre-United States. Charley, Belle, Luzena, Ah Toy, Mary Ellen, Lola, Lotta, and Madame Moustache benefit from the results of these atrocities. Our state, and country, who claims to be a leader in morality, STILL benefit from the results of these atrocities. Resources and land, stolen.

The gold extracted from the Native's cherished lands, funded this powerful nation and kickstarted its wealth. The price? Genocide. The basement of the United States is flooded with the blood and the tears of Native people whose only crime was living in their own country, and therefore stood in the way of an invasion. Human life is never irrelevant. Until the Story of the hunt is told by the Lion, the tale of the hunt will always glorify the hunter.

Until recently, "conflict history" has been dismissed. We then miss important lessons that are absolutely necessary for understanding our American history. It is time we incorporate racial and ethnic conflict when we view the American experience, or we will never understand how far we have come and how far we have to go. No matter how painful it may be, we can only move forward by accepting the truth. Frontier pioneer Eliza Inman wrote in her journal in 1843, "*If Hell laid to the West, Americans would cross Heaven to reach it.*" It looks like she was right.

The End

Acknowledgments

I have an unlimited source of gratitude for my family and friends who have stayed by my side as I continue this journey. Thank you for the friendship you provided and the sacrifices you made while I dug my nose in the books. *Sailor, Waylon, Bella, Mom, Matt, Zac, Brandon, Natalie, Sarah, Jess, Mysti, Kai and Gannon.*

To the rest of the people who had my back, and always supported me and my wild decisions, I appreciate you. *Shasta, Carly, Cara M, Nikki C, Jodi S, Charles & Mary, Carly F, Johan Ms, Andrea Alicia, Amie Astelle, Jack Gibson, James Pellegrini, J.D Wilkes, Bob Wayne, Lester Raww, Miss Savvy, Michael Miller, Kyrsten Johnson, Sarah S, Cara M, Teresa Torbett at Columbia Mercantile 1855, Sean Woodbridge, Mary Cowper and Def & Ann.* Thank you to *Slim Cessna & DBUK* for your gracious contribution to the podcast episodes.

This work was done in memory of Linda Berry (Gigi), *Kym Berry-Andrews, Joaquin Acuna, Max Delacy, Greg Noll, Lavonne Hill, Virginia Anderson and Brian Anderson. Miss you.*

Resources

- Abeloe, William N Rensch "Historic Spots In California" 2002 ISBN-10: 9780804744836

- Allende, Isabel "Daughter of Fortune" Harper Perennial, May 2, 2006 ISBN-10: 9780061120251

- Americanhistory.si.edu

- Arango, Tim "Overlooked No More: Charley Parkhurst, Gold Rush Legend With a Hidden Identity" for NY Times Dec 5, 2018

- Bancroft, Hubert Howe "History of California; Volume 2" Franklin Classics, October 13, 2018 ISBN-10: 0342896423

- Barnhart, Jacqueline Baker "Working Women: Prostitution in San Francisco from the Gold Rush to 1900" University of California, Santa Cruz, 1976

- Beyl, Ernest "A short history of bordellos in San Francisco" for Marina Times April 2012

- Bodiehistory.com

- Bitesizehistory.net

- Blakemore, Erin "The Enslaved Natives that made the Gold Rush Possible" for History.com

- Blea, Irene I. "Forgotten Lynching Victims - Mexicans in America - U.S. Chicanas and Latinas in a Historical Context"

- The Bodie Standard News Oct. 9, 1880

- Breider, Sophie, "The Best Bad Things": An Analytical History of the Madams of Gold Rush San Francisco" (2017). CMC Senior Theses.

- Bristow, Kathi "Those Daring Stage Drivers" Interpretation and Education Division California State Parks, 2008

- Burr, Charles Chauncey "Lectures Of Lola Montez" Nabu Press, November 3, 2011 ISBN-10: 1271050803

- Campbell, Augustus, and Colin D. Campbell. "Crossing the Isthmus of Panama, 1849 the Letters of Dr. Augustus Campbell." California History 78, no. 4 (1999)

- Cannon, Michael "Montez, Lola" (1821-1861 for Australian Dictionary of Biography, Volume 5, 1974

- Carlsson, Chris "Mary Ellen Pleasant" for Foundsf.org 2007

- Carrigan, William D. and Webb, Clive "When Americans Lynched Mexicans" for NYtimes.com 2015

- Chambers, Veronica "The Many Chapters Of Mary Ellen Pleasant" for NY Times Overlooked

- Circadian, Robin "Bloody Islands: A Collection of Stories Relating to the Bloody Island Massacre of 1850" September 6, 2013

- Cliff, Michelle "Free Enterprise: A Novel of Mary Ellen Pleasant" City Lights Publishers, September 1, 2004 ISBN-10: 0872864375

- Cohn, Julia G. "The Showgirl Full of Sin or Respectable Theatre? The Gold Rush Performer as a Western Woman?: Lola Montez Capitalizes On Gold Rush Popular Culture In Flux"

- Cui, Candace "Badass Ladies Of Chinese History: Ah Toy"

- Daniel, Judy "Bodie: The Golden Years" March 9, 2012 ISBN-10: 0615574270
- Death Valley Days TV Series (1952-1970)
- Deerhollowfarmfriends.org

- Dickson, Samuel "Tales of San Francisco" Stanford University Press; January 1, 1968

- Dimuro, Gina "How Lola Montez Seduced 19th-Century Europe's Most Famous Men — And Even Took Down A King" for Allthatsiinteresting.com
- Downie, Major William "Hunting for Gold" Sylvanite Publishing January 29, 2016 ISBN-10: 1614740887

- Dwyer, Jeff "Ghost Hunter's Guide to California's Gold Rush Country" Pelican October 12, 2009 ISBN-10: 1589806875
- Elk Grove Historical Society Elk Grove, California "Stagecoach Driver: Charley Parkhurst"
- Encyclopedia.com

- Enss, Chris "Love Lessons from the Old West: Wisdom From Wild Women" Globe Pequot Press January 14, 2014

- Enss, Chris "Wicked Women: Notorious, Mischievous, and Wayward Ladies from the Old West" TwoDot February 20, 2015

- Farrier, Nancy J. "Pretty Juanita" food Hhhistory.com
- Foundsf.org

- Fraizer, Laurie "The White Woman's Burden Chinese Prostitution in San Francisco"

- Gregory, Kristiana "Madame Mustache and the Boys of Bodie" KK Publishing Corp February 15, 2015 ISBN-10: 098615220X

- Guzman, Andrea "Living on Ohlone Land" November 20th, 2018 for Oaklandlibrary.org

- Hall, Daniel M. "The Strange Life And Times Of Charley Parkhurst." Metro Santa Cruz. 2003-03-05. SCPL Local History.

- Halley, Marian "Don't Call Her Mammy" for Newfillmore.com 2012

- Harris, Gloria G. "By Women Trailblazers of California: Pioneers to the Present" The History Press August 7, 2012 ISBN-10: 1609496752

- Hauck, William Dennis "Haunted Places: The National Directory: Ghostly Abodes, Sacred Sites, UFO Landings and Other Supernatural Locations" Penguin Books Updated edition August 27, 2002 ISBN-10: 0142002348

- Heichelbech, Rose "The Spider Dance That Captivated the World in the 1840s" for dustyoldthing.com

- Henry, Fern "My Checkered Life. Luzena Stanley Wilson in Early California" Carl Mautz Publishing January 1, 2003 ISBN-10: 1887694536
- Historicallyhot.com

- Holliday, J. S. "The World Rushed In: The California Gold Rush Experience" University of Oklahoma Press December 9, 2002 ISBN-10: 080613464X

- Hudson, Lynn M. "The Making of "Mammy Pleasant": A Black Entrepreneur in Nineteenth-Century San Francisco (Women, Gender, and Sexuality in American History)" University of Illinois Press January 10, 2008 ISBN-10: 0252075277
- Indiancountrytoday.com
- Indians.org

- Johnson, Susan Lee, Ph.D. "Roaring Camp: The Social World of the California Gold Rush" W. W. Norton & Company; Reprint edition December 17, 2000 ISBN-10: 0393320995

- Kamiya, Gary "San Francisco's Chinatown Was a Seedy Ghetto." Feb. 22, 2019 for San Francisco Chronicle

- Kelly, Kate "Mary Ellen Pleasant, Entrepreneur and Abolitionist Black Leaders, Heroes & Trailblazers" for americacomesalive.com
- Kohler, Hannah "The Tale of Josefa"
- Kondazian, Karen (2012) The Whip, Hansen Publishing Group, ISBN-10: 978-1601823021

- Kroeber, A. L. "Handbook of the Indians of California, Smithsonian Institution, Bureau of American Ethnology, Bulletin No. 78" Dover Publications February 29, 2012 ISBN-10: 0486233685
- KQED.org
- Lapp, Rudolph M. "Blacks in Gold Rush California (The Lamar Series in Western History)" September 10, 1977
- Legendsofamerica.com
- Levy, Jo Ann "Daughter of Joy: A Novel of Gold Rush California (Women of the West)" Forge January 1, 1998 ISBN-10: 0312865023
- Levy, Jo Ann "They Saw the Elephant" OU Press September 5, 2014 ISBN-10: 0806124733
- Library of Congress, National Digital Library Program: American Memory Project "California as I Saw It": First-Person Narratives of California's Early Years, 1849-1900
- Lindahl, Steve "Living in a Star's Light: A novel based on the life of Miss Lotta Crabtree" August 1, 2019 ISBN-10: 0578554828
- MacDonald, Craig "Cockeyed Charley Parkhurst: The West's Most Unusual Stage Whip" Colorado: Filter Press, 1973
- Madley, Benjamin "An American Genocide: The United States and the California Indian Catastrophe 1846-1873" Yale University Press May 24, 2016
- Marinatimes.com
- Maritimeheritage.org
- Margolin, Malcolm "The Ohlone Way: Indian Life in the San Francisco-Monterey Bay Area" Heyday August 1, 1978 ISBN-10: 0930588010
- The Maritime Heritage Project ~ Maritime Nations, Ship Passengers: 1846-1899
- Marryat, Frank "Mountains and Molehills: Or Recollections from a Burnt Journal" Skyhorse June 3, 2014 ISBN-10: 1628737352
- Mcgraw, Jainie "The Gold Rush Character Analysis"
- Mendoza, Charlie "The Ohlone (Spotlight on the American Indians of California)" PowerKids Press January 15, 2018 ISBN-10: 1538324830
- Mewuk.com
- Mirandé, Alfredo and Enríquez, Evangelina "La Chicana: The Mexican-American Woman" University of Chicago Press March 15, 1981 ISBN-10: 0226531600

- Montez, Lola "The Arts Of Beauty; Or, Secrets Of A Lady's Toilet - With Hints To Gentlemen On The Art Of Fascinating" Baltzell Press July 24, 2009 ISBN-10: 1444646540
- Montoliu, Raphael "Lucy Moore Foundation Seeks To Create Healing, Understanding" for Lake County News, August 25, 2007
- Murfin, Patrick "Bad Day on Bloody Island – or Just Another Massacre", Heretic, Rebel, A Thing to Flout (blog) May, 15 2014
- Muwekma.org
- Nahc.ca.gov - The California Native American Heritage Commission
- Ojibwa, "California's War on Indians" for Native American Netroots (blog) March 2, 2015
- The Oldest Profession Podcast theoldestprofessionpodcast.com
- Outland, Charles F. "Stagecoaching on El Camino Real, Los Angeles to San Francisco, 1861-1901" The Arthur H. Clark Company January 1, 1973 ISBN-10: 0870621068
- Parker, John PhD "Heizer's 1973 Collected Documents on the Causes and Events of the Bloody Island Massacre of 1850"
- Parker, John PhD "The Kelsey Brothers: A California Disaster" - Presented at the 2012 November meeting of the Lake County Historical Society
- Payne, Lee "Tales from the Mountain of Gold: A Chinese Slave Girl in Gold Rush San Francisco" CreateSpace Independent Publishing Platform January 16, 2012 ISBN-10: 1468041894
- PBS The Gold Rush Impact on Native Tribes: From the Collection: NATIVE AMERICANS & The Land of Gold and Hope, PBS Interactive
- Piatt, Michael H. "The Death of Madame Mustache: Bodie's Most Celebrated Inhabitant" March 2009
- Piatt, Michael H. "The Bad Man from Bodie" September 2007
- Placzek, Jessica "Meet Charley Parkhurst: the Gold Rush's Fearless, Gender Nonconforming Stagecoach Driver" April 25, 2019, KQED
- Pleasant, Rosa "Equality Before The Law" for coloredconventions.org/
- Pryor, Alton "Fascinating Women in California History" Stagecoach Publishing January 16, 2014 ISBN-10: 0966005392

- Pryor, Alton The Bawdy House Girls" CreateSpace Independent Publishing Platform January 21, 2014 ISBN-10: 1495238180

- Radin, Max and Benson, William Ralganal "The Stone and Kelsey "Massacre" on the Shores of Clear Lake in 1849: The Indian Viewpoint" California Historical Society Quarterly (1932)

- Richards, Rand "Mud, Blood and Gold: San Francisco in 1849" Heritage House October 7, 2008 ISBN-10: 1879367068

- Roberts, Sylvia Alden "Mining for Freedom: Black History Meets the California Gold Rush" iUniverse November 4, 2008 ISBN-10: 0595524923

- Ross, Louie "Native Americans: American History: An Overview of "Native American History" - Your Guide To: Native People, Indians, & Indian History" April 30, 2016

- Rourke, Constance Mayfield "Troupers of the Gold Coast: The Rise of Lotta Crabtree" Skyhorse Publishing January 1, 2016 ISBN-10: 1634506820

- Sarris, Greg "The Last Woman From Petaluma" September 29, 2016 for California State Library
- Sequoiaparksconservancy.org

- Seymour, Bruce "Lola Montez: A Life" Yale University Press, New Haven & London September 4, 2009 ISBN-10: 0300074395
- SF ARGUS Newspaper, 1855 Editions
- SFmuseum.org

- Sinn, Elizabeth "Pacific Crossing: California Gold, Chinese Migration, and the Making of Hong Kong" Hong Kong University Press; Reprint edition December 1, 2012 ISBN-10: 988813972X

- Smith, Stacey L. "Freedom's Frontier California and the Struggle over Unfree Labor, Emancipation, and Reconstruction" University of North Carolina Press August 1, 2015 ISBN-10: 1469626535

- Snyder-Reinke, Jeffrey "Cradle to Grave - Baby Towers and the Politics of Infant Burial in Qing China" The College of Idaho for Chinesedeathscape.org

- Soule, Frank "The Annals of San Francisco" Berkeley Hills Books January 1, 1998 ISBN-10: 096537744X

- The Sovereign Hill Museums Association "Lola Montez and her Notorious Spider Dance" for Culture Victoria

- Sowards, Adam M. "The Legacy of Lynching in the West for High Country News July 13, 2018

- Sparkletack Podcast - sparkletack.com

- Stoddard, Lothrop "The Rising Tide of Color Against White World-Supremacy: The Worldview of an American Eugenicist & Ku Klux Klan Historian" e-artnow June 18, 2020

- Swain, William "Life in the California Gold Fields" 1850 Digital History ID 1194
- Sweetheartsofthewest.com
- Theautry.org
- Thebellecora.com
- Theparisreview.org

- Trafzer, Clifford E. "Exterminate Them: Written Accounts of the Murder, Rape, and Enslavement of Native Americans during the California Gold Rush" Michigan State University Press 1999 ISBN-10: 0870135015

- Varley, James F. "Lola Montez: The California Adventures of Europe's Notorious Courtesan" The Arthur H. Clark Company February 13, 1996

- Varney, Philip & Hinckley Jim "Ghost Towns of the West" Voyageur Press April 11, 2017 ISBN-10: 0760350418

- Wagner, Tricia Martineau "African American Women of the Old West" TwoDot February 1, 2007

- Wills, Shomari "Black Fortunes: The Story of the First Six African Americans Who Survived Slavery and Became Millionaires" Amistad January 29, 2019 ISBN-10: 0062437607

- White, Richard "Naming America's Own Genocide" for The Nation August, 2016

- Wiles, Gary "Femmes Fatales, Gamblers, Yankees And Rebels in the Gold Fields 1859-1869" Photosensitive June 30, 2005 ISBN-10: 1889252131
- Wilson, Luzena Stanley, and Wilson Wright, Correnah.

Luzena Stanley Wilson "'49er: memories" Mills College, Calif. The Eucalyptus press, 1937.
- Womenhistoryblog.com
- Worldhistory.us

-Wyckoff, Bob "The French Lady Was A Gambler!" for The Union News for Nevada County, California May 11, 2011

Made in the USA
Las Vegas, NV
09 February 2024